Amanda Prantera was born and
She went for a brief holiday to Italy when she was twenty and has lived there ever since. She is married with two daughters. Her short-story collection **Proto Zoë** was serialised on BBC Radio's **Woman's Hour. The Young Italians** is her fifth novel.

By the same Author

Strange Loop
The Cabalist
Conversations with Lord Byron
On Perversion, 163 Years After
His Lordship's Death
The Side of the Moon
Proto Zoë

THE YOUNG ITALIANS

Amanda Prantera

First published 1993

1 3 5 7 9 10 8 6 4 2

First published by Bloomsbury Publishing Ltd in 1993,
2 Soho Square, London W1V 5DE

This edition published by Arrow in 1994

Arrow Books Limited
Random House UK Ltd, 20 Vauxhall Bridge Road, London SW1V 2SA

Random House Australia (Pty) Limited
20 Alfred Street, Milsons Point, Sydney,
New South Wales 2061, Australia

Random House New Zealand Limited
18 Poland Road, Glenfield
Auckland 10, New Zealand

Random House South Africa (Pty) Limited
PO Box 337, Bergvlei, South Africa

Random House UK Limited Reg. No. 954009

A CIP catalogue record for this book
is available from the British Library

ISBN 0 09 937701 2

Printed and bound in Great Britain by
Cox & Wyman Ltd, Reading, Berkshire

To Sophie

CHAPTER I

Many years later, when her Italian life had a historical flavour to it even for her, Irene was to be questioned by an architect she met at a dinner party about the railway station in Florence. And with some insistence. 'You arrived there in the winter of 1928, Mrs Fortini, is that right?' he said. 'How interesting. Then it would have been the old, original building that you saw, before Mussolini got to work on it and tarted it up to fit the Fascist image. How splendid, how absolutely fascinating.' From the fervour with which he spoke he evidently had more than a conversational interest in the matter. '*Do* tell me what it looked like, I can't wait to hear.'

But of course she had to disappoint the man, because apart from a boy with a tray hung round his neck containing curious little dried fruits wrapped in silver paper, as pretty and decorative as charms to be worn on a bracelet, she remembered nothing.

Nothing, that is, but a sense of loneliness so burning and acute that, had there been a hole for her to hide in, she would have crept into it and never come out again, not even if lured by hunger and the enticing scent of the fruits.

Although she was accustomed to being on her own, this sensation was new to her. It had been largely provoked by her travelling companions' reactions during the journey. Time after time, ever since the train had crossed the border with France, people had got into the carriage where she was sitting, and, after eyeing her for a while with sympathetic but evidently irrepressible curiosity, had asked her, *scusi tanto*, but what on earth was she doing – a young, nicely brought up Signorina like herself – alone, on a train? Didn't her parents know that it was dangerous, unseemly, for a young woman to travel alone?

Each time, patiently, in her textbook Italian, Irene had trotted out the answer for them, explaining as best as she could and as undramatically (she had rapidly come to dread the looks of shocked commiseration which she knew would shortly appear on her listeners' faces) that her parents were past caring about such matters, having died when she was a child; that her grandmother too, by whom she had been brought up, was also beyond caring, having died the previous week; that, no, she had no brothers or sisters, and that she was journeying to Florence to take up residence with her only living relative, an aunt, who lived in that city and had done so for many years. (Although strictly speaking, of course, Aunt Frances was only a half-aunt, being half-sister to Irene's mother, but this it had seemed unnecessary, and rather difficult from a linguistic point of view, to point out.)

Unfailingly the listeners had brightened towards the end of the explanation and latched on to the last codicil. An aunt, they had said, relieved. *Una zia. Ah, bene, bene, bene.* And no doubt this aunt would be coming to meet her niece at the station? Of course she would, and everything would then be as it should be: a family reunion, however reduced in size. But while saying this they also unfailingly managed to convey a residual sense of disapproval: Italian parents, they implied, even from the other side of the grave would still have managed to fix some kind of escort for their only daughter. One of them, a young man in the black uniform of the Fascist militia who was travelling all the way to Florence, made the reproof quite explicit. Yes, he murmured dubiously at the end of Irene's story, looking down at his scarred but highly polished boots. That was as maybe. But no self-respecting Italian family would ever allow a girl of – how old was the Signorina if he might ask? Nineteen. Ayee! That was even younger than he thought – a girl of nineteen to travel all the way across Europe on her own the way she was doing now. He did not know quite how they would have managed it if they were all dead, but he knew that someone would have thought of something. Probably the aunt herself would have made the journey, that was it. Both ways, and been pleased to do so.

Hard as she tried to throw him off, the young man insisted on hanging about Irene when they arrived in Florence, and it was in fact he who, when it appeared clear that Aunt Frances had not even been pleased to make the short trip from her flat to the station to meet her orphaned niece, carried her luggage to the exit for her and found her a taxi. Deepening the shame she already felt at being so culpably, so offensively kinless in this country where kinship appeared to be the corner-stone of everything, Irene could see his intentions towards her changing. On the train he had been respectful, almost smarmy. On the platform he was still helpful, although she could already feel him giving her some funny sideways glances when he thought she wasn't looking, and brushing her hand with his on purpose/by mistake as they grappled with the suitcases. But by the time they reached the taxi rank, where a dusty collection of horse-drawn cabs and motor vehicles was lined up waiting for hire, he seemed to have decided that her unclaimed status made her available merchandise, and had taken such a firm and possessive grip of her arm that she had difficulty shaking herself free and persuading the driver to draw away. The man – another disbeliever in lone female travel – quite naturally assumed she and the young Fascist were together.

More embarrassment, therefore, and more unwarranted feelings of guilt as she explained to the disappointed cab driver that this was not the case. But he too, like all the others, perked up when he learnt where she was directed. '*Casa della zia*!' he said, giving a wide smile and flicking his whip lightly over the horse's rump to set the animal in motion. To Auntie's house. As if, Irene thought to herself unconvinced, the address she had given him were that of a world-famous sanatorium where all her ills would be cured.

CHAPTER II

Aunt Frances's dark, frowzy, inhospitable flat in Florence did not turn out to be a place of cure for any of Irene's ills. Not in itself, that is. It was, true, the place from which the cure was first attempted, but since the attempt was fortuitous and stemmed mostly from her own overwhelming desire to leave the place and her aunt's almost equally strong desire to see her leave, she was never inclined to attribute much therapeutic merit to the building. Yet, despite being almost constantly uncomfortable in one way or another during the three months that she spent inside it, she always thought back on the flat in via Giuseppe Giusti with a certain fondness.

And also with unusual clarity. She remembered, no, nothing of the railway station's architecture on her arrival, nothing of the streets as she drove through them, nothing of the people who thronged them (or perhaps didn't, seeing that the one thing she did seem to recall was that it was desperately cold). Even the villa at Forte dei Marmi, which was to be her world, her underworld and paradise for the next ten years, had its dark spots in her memory, its fuzzy areas, its blanks. In contrast, every detail of her aunt's apartment, and particularly of the famous *salotto* into which she was ushered as soon as she set foot in the flat (without, to her dismay, even being asked if she wanted to wash her hands after the journey), stayed clearly in Irene's mind ever afterwards. So clearly in fact that almost half a century later she was able to instruct the executors of her aunt's will over the telephone as to which pieces of furniture and stuff to set aside for her and which to sell.

The reason for this inventorial precision she never could quite fathom. Admittedly Aunt Frances strove for effect in her décor, fashioning, as each Wednesday came round, elaborate 'conversation pieces' out of peacock feathers and hookas, planting tubs of smouldering joss-sticks in every corner and swathing the rather grubby furnishings with lengths of crimped Fortuny silk in purple and apricot and flame (reminders, she confided archly to Irene, of her daring past when she had indulged in the titillating pursuit of 'skirt dancing'. Very *passé* now, of course, but what art, what grace there had been in striking up a pose and twitching the draperies so that they rippled and shimmered round the form, revealing just the right amount of ankle!). Admittedly, too, there was plenty of time for observation, because Aunt Frances, for the first five or six weeks anyway, before dissatisfaction set in on her side as well, took the task of making her niece feel at home very literally, and as sole concession to outdoor entertainment took her once to the Uffizi and once to the Medici tombs, which were shut. But even allowing for both these factors it seemed amazing to Irene that her dormant nineteen-year-old mind should have registered, and so tenaciously, such minutiae as the patterns of the carving on the back of her aunt's chairs and the flecks and spirals in her collection of glass paperweights. Perhaps time, like space, was bendable, and because something remarkable was *about* to happen to her but had not yet happened, her memory had looped round afterwards and caught the prelude, investing it with a significance it did not as yet possess.

Except, if that were so, then it would presumably be the latter period she remembered best, immediately before the remarkable happening took place, whereas it was in fact the evening of her arrival that was etched most vividly of all, with a decided tapering off of clearness as the weeks progressed and the day of deliverance drew near. She could see, almost as if she had a film-recording of it inside her head to play and freeze and replay at will, the dramatic, smoky room, with its undramatic, smoky occupants, ill at ease against the carefully constructed backcloth of exotica. (Ill at ease, too, in their actual physical positions, for Aunt Frances encouraged her guests to recline on poufs or cushions *à la Turque*, and punished the unadventurous by providing hard, upright chairs in Renaissance style as the only alternative.) She could see the cushion destined for herself, midway between the lady oboist and the breeder of cocker spaniels – roan cocker spaniels, blue roan, she even remembered the colour. She could see the dusty brocade curtains, the rows upon rows of ill-framed water-colours in her aunt's hesitant hand, could hear the clatter of the glasses and tea things and the desultory English voices raised above it, most of them uttering vaguely carping remarks about the country they had chosen, or been obliged, by the sound of it, to live in. The Italians this, the Italians that; so cliquey, so uppity nowadays, so hard to meet the 'right' ones. Everything so dear, nothing as it used to be. Good tea so hard to come by, where *did* Frances manage to find this delicious Earl Grey? Musso getting tiresome, servants getting bolshie; no marmalade, no decent mustard, no suet; thinking of packing it in and going somewhere one could make a proper garden. On they droned, on they quibbled. And in the midst of the drone, cutting through it and leaving a rent behind it which the other voices were quick to close over, she could hear the voice of the one American present, the estranged wife of some obscure Florentine count or other, proclaiming with apostolic zeal, 'Well, you lot can say what you like, but with me Mussolini comes before Gawd, before Gawd!'

Yes, it always struck Irene as strange, this wealth of detail cropped from an evening that had wearied her to the point of exhaustion. She could even remember the exact look on her aunt's face as she listened to the American woman's outburst: a look of pure and almost childish delight, sharpened by a hunting dog's alertness on scenting game. Not, as Irene had first thought, on account of the pro-Fascist opinion expressed, because the English-speaking contingent was mostly critical of the Duce and Aunt Frances had immediately intervened in quality of hostess to reprimand her guest with a raised finger and a 'Now, now, Lula, don't be naughty, don't provoke!' meaning just the opposite, but on account of the animation it brought (or might hopefully have brought, had the provocation worked) to her cherished *salotto*. By which term, Irene gradually came to realize over the coming weeks, Aunt Frances did not mean to refer to the room, so much as the event taking place inside it, using the word in the similar but by no means equivalent French sense of *salon*, and picturing herself to herself with Quixotic disregard of reality as a latterday trans-Alpine version of Madame du Deffand.

All this, it had taken Irene time to understand. Time and distance, and the tolerance that both these dimensions bring when properly deployed. Cooped up with her aunt in the minute over-furnished apartment, on what to both of them had as then threatened to be a more or less permanent basis, these foibles had not appeared sympathetic to her in the least. That first Wednesday evening, what with tiredness and bewilderment and a persistent and ever growing desire to go to the lavatory which shyness had prevented her from making known, she had suffered agonies. And worse agonies were to come as the dreary routine of the *salotto*, and preparation for the *salotto*, and clearing up after the *salotto* and talking about the last one and speculating about the next, repeated itself, day after day and week after week: for, having set aside her paintbrushes, all Aunt Frances's creative energies seemed to centre on this one event, this one production. Much later, however, when such ordeals were a thing of the past, Irene could look back on the determined six-foot figure of her aunt as it surged from its cushions, encouraging, gesticulating, trying desperately to wrench some sparks from the obstinately sparkless guests, and recognize that it had a noble, almost heroic quality about it.

But this was another epoch, and another Irene judging. At the time she merely felt exasperation. As, too, eventually and thankfully, did Aunt Frances herself. On – Irene had almost lost count but she reckoned it must have been the morning of the sixth Wednesday, or possibly the seventh, she went into the kitchen where she had been bidden as usual to help out with the sandwich cutting, to find her aunt busy consulting the telephone directory, a list of names and numbers at her elbow. From the long-suffering look on her face as she scrutinized the pages, it seemed to Irene she was making, or was about to make, or had just made, a great effort on somebody else's behalf.

The list was slid smartly under the directory when Irene approached, but then her aunt seemed to change her mind and drew it out again, still keeping it well covered by the sleeve of her kimono. Seeing, she announced a little huffily, that last Wednesday she had given her niece one of the best-placed cushions, next to dear Miss Wood and that *fascinating* man who made the hand-painted wrapping paper, and all Irene had done in return was to curl up on the cushion and doze, she had decided to organize for her some alternative form of entertainment for this evening. By which both Irene and the *salotto* would benefit: great sleepy girls who made no effort were not exactly an asset to any gathering, did she realize? No, no, she went on more kindly, there was no need to apologize, not everyone was cut out for cosmopolitan, adult society and evidently Irene was missing the company of people of her own age. It was quite natural that she should. There was no need to get excited either, because finding what she was looking for was not going to be an easy task. She had already telephoned her lawyer who had a son roughly the right age, *and* her doctor, *and* several friends of friends, but as yet there had been no takers. Italian parents were so weird when it came to lending out their offspring, they treated one quite like a kidnapper. The young man must be dependable, of course, and preferably have the use of a car. Although he and Irene could, she supposed, do their sight-seeing and whatnot perfectly well on foot. But, no, on second thoughts a car would be better: like that they could go further afield and stay out later and not come back until the *salotto* was well and truly over.

Thus it was that Tommaso came into Irene's life. Or to put it more accurately, because she could hardly claim to have had much of a life of her own before she met him, thus it was that she came into his. The web-thin steel-strong threads of destiny. Or the web-thin steel-strong tendrils of chance. A few days before she left the flat for good, while looking for the number of the Consulate to ask about the banns, she happened to come across the mysterious list of names lying between the pages of the telephone directory, and noticed that her aunt had in fact cast her net fairly wide before settling on this particular candidate. There was, as to be expected, Aunt Frances's lawyer's name and number, crossed out, with the words 'No go' beside it; there was her doctor's, with another stroke through it and the injunction to herself 'Try locum later'; and underneath these there was a whole string of other names which Irene did not recognize, most of them also cancelled and bearing negative comments like 'Too old', 'Too busy', 'Drawn another blank'. But interspersed with the crossed-out names there were several uncrossed, with question-marks and ticks to them and remarks like 'Good poss.' and 'Likely starter' and 'Will do at a pinch'. And there was one, she remembered, not only ticked but starred and heavily encircled and marked 'Sounds just the job. Call again next Mon. eve.' What chain of events, guided or random, she sometimes wondered, had brought her Tommaso instead of one of these other more or less suitable, more or less available young men? A lucky one, that was all she could say. An unbelievably lucky one. Especially when, alone of all the names, Tommaso's had nothing beside it at all. And especially, too, when in the rudderless state she was in she would most probably have taken anyone, allowed herself to be taken by anyone: old or busy or very slight poss. indeed.

Aunt Frances, of course, when she saw what was happening and what her somewhat slapdash manipulations with the telephone directory had brought about, did not look on it as a fortunate occurrence at all. It was one thing to have her niece taken off her hands for an evening so that the *salotto* could better blossom in her absence; it was quite another to have her spirited away for good. By the son of a chemist, what was more, and not even a laboratory chemist but one who stood behind a counter and wrapped up sanitary towels – no, not sanitary towels, because you couldn't get them in this wretched country, but cotton wool and pills and worse. When Irene reeled in, late and dishevelled, after her first outing (it was common knowledge, Tommaso told her later, that any girl who stepped voluntarily into a car in Italy alone with a man was considered fair game: he was surprised her aunt should not have known this after living in the country for so long), Aunt Frances bent absorbedly over her tapestry and made no comment other than to say she hoped her niece had not found the outing tiring. To which Irene had been obliged to reply, untruthfully because her entire body was aching with strain and fatigue, that she had not. But when, as he did, being very forthright and bulldozery in his approach to life, Tommaso started calling for Irene every day of the week, not only Wednesdays, and coming to the door of the flat to collect her, and barging his way inside armed with flowers and presents for both niece and aunt, and issuing formal invitations for them to dine with his family and goodness knows what other enticements, Aunt Frances began to hedge. And to urge her niece to do the same.

'You know what all this means, Irene dear?' she said, indicating the most recent consignment of orchids and marrons glacés. 'It means the little fellow is serious, bless his heart.' (Tommaso stood at five foot eleven which in those days was tall, especially for an Italian, so by the 'little' it was clear to Irene that a more general disparagement of his qualities was intended. Even without the 'bless', which was uttered more with the venom of 'cuss'.) 'And this in turn means we will have to be very firm with him if we are to avoid unpleasantness. For Miss Wood's sake, who is a friend of the family and put me on to them in the first place, we will accept one invitation to a meal – not dinner, though, I think; lunch would be better – and then, softly, softly, *during* lunch if the occasion arises, we will make our position clear. *Nix nisba*, as the Italians say. No tripe for pussycats. Nothing doing. Come to think of it, you could even start doing a little distancing on your own account this evening by telling him you have a headache and cannot go out with him in that vulgar great car.'

But by then it was of course too late for distancing, either on Irene's part or anyone else's. It was not that she had made up her mind, nothing so resolute; it was simply that, almost without her noticing it, somebody else appeared to have stepped in and made it up for her. As she was later to discover, the German/Tuscan grafting in her future husband's pedigree made a formidable mixture when it came to will-power. Despite Aunt

Frances's increasing coldness each time he came to call at the flat, despite her truly icy behaviour at the family lunch-party (greatly admired by the elder relatives who found it *molto distinto, molto inglese*), despite her endless warnings to Irene that by marrying a chemist's son she would be signing her social death warrant, cutting herself off entirely from the Florentine nobility and the English colony alike, and even – the ultimate disgrace – risking permanent exclusion from the *salotto*; despite all this Irene, guided by the as yet imperceptible nudge of the bulldozer, went on treading her steady sleepwalker's path towards the altar. Obtaining certificates, choosing organ music, ordering flowers, enduring Tommaso's taurine assaults in the car (which at present seemed to be the only price she had to pay for whatever it was she was getting), and reminding herself, if ever she stopped to question her progress, which she seldom did, that at least she was moving towards someone who appeared to want her, who seemed to have some idea, however basic, of what to do with her, and that anyway it would be silly to start having doubts and kicking up a fuss because, apart from the flat and the endless treadmill of the *salottos*, she had nowhere else to go and nothing else of a particularly pressing nature to do.

Not the best reasons, perhaps, for entering into an irrevocable life-long contract with a recently met foreigner (there was no divorce in Italy in those days, as Aunt Frances constantly reminded her, reading out grisly stories from the newspapers about uxoricide and disillusioned brides whose hair fell out at a single shedding on their wedding night), but reasons. Early in the spring of 1929, three months after she had set foot on Italian soil, in the presence of eighty-nine smiling guests of his and one sulky one of hers, Irene and Tommaso were married, and that, for the time being anyway, was that. Miss Wood was also invited on the bride's side, but developed a bad cold on the eve and could not come. Which perhaps, Irene could not help thinking as she caught sight of the funeral-like veil her aunt had chosen to wear for the ceremony, was all for the best.

CHAPTER III

Another of Aunt Frances's dire warnings, often coupled with an even direr one about Italians (and especially German-Italians) having no proper sense of humour: 'Remember, Irene, that if you marry an Italian you do not marry a man but a family.'

This last prediction turned out to be true, to an extent that not even Aunt Frances herself in her worst imaginings could have foreseen. Although more than a family, the group of people of which she was now a member seemed to Irene to constitute a clan, a tribe, almost a small nation. Fortunately peace-loving and well disposed towards her, in spite of the fact (zestfully explained to her by Assunta, the most senior of the maids) that she brought with her no trousseau to display to female visitors, had only one relative and a snooty one at that, and was known to have spent most of the time of her courtship alone with Tommaso in the scandalous confines of the family car. (So scandalous in fact that, still according to Assunta, the upholstery of the vehicle had had to be wiped down with holy water before the aunts would consent to ride in it without their gloves on.)

At the wedding her head had swum with names and faces, had ached with the effort of trying to attach the one to the other: Aunt Pussi, Aunt Lise, Aunt This, Uncle That, Cousin Whatnot – German cousin (whatever that was, it appeared to be something more than a question of nationality) to Cousin Someone Else who was married to the tall woman in red she had just been introduced to and whose name was gone already; the old woman with the kind crinkly face who had kissed her fingertips and called her *Liebling* (a real German relation this time?); the other one – sister? Sister-in-law? Twin? They looked alike as two dried peas – who had knocked Aunt Frances speechless by telling her she had studied English in her youth with a princess from Liverpool. ('Such a sainty lady, Mrs Frances, you would never believe, she teach us to say all the time Jesus Christ! Jesus Christ!') The charming, fey-looking peroxide-blonde who had clasped Irene's hand feelingly and proffered matrimonial counsel should she need it. The fat, jolly man who ate so much Aunt Frances couldn't take her eyes off him; the thin gaunt man who ate even more. Irene had despaired of ever being able to sort them all out. She couldn't even tell the close relatives from the distant ones because by the way they all behaved together there didn't seem to *be* any distant ones. She was afraid she would forever be forced to give offence by muddling them up and forgetting who they were and how they fitted in.

They were gentle, considerate people, however, with a sense of loyalty towards Tommaso that in the elder members amounted almost to hero-worship, and to begin with they left Irene alone in her new apartment at the top of the family tenement as if sensing her need for time in which to acclimatize. Merely intruding on her privacy indirectly with presents of food sent up by maids, and messages of goodwill in spidery Gothic hands, and pots of cacti tied up in ribbons. In this way, by making separate little thank-you sorties at intervals and repeating her findings to Tommaso when he came home from work in the evenings to make sure she had got things right, Irene was able to draw up a kind of skeleton family-tree in her head showing roots and trunk and principal branches, which would stand her in good stead later on when the family moved to its summer residence of Forte dei Marmi and everyone and everything got mixed up again.

The tree was a beguilingly simple one, she found (provided you went back to grandparent-level and stuck to the German side, which perhaps a little surprisingly was the side that even now held the family together): there was the branch founded by Tommaso's grandfather Edmund, to which she herself now belonged, and three other branches, founded by his three sisters, Lise, Pussi and Tita. And that was all: one German-based trunk, four *émigré* German branches, each with its array of Italian branchlets and twiglets attached. It should have been easy, therefore, when trying to place any present member of the family, simply to slot whoever it was into one of these four groups, but alas it wasn't: partly because Edmund and Lise had muddled things up from the start by marrying siblings – Savia and the German-sounding Otto (who was in fact one hundred per cent Italian and insisted that his name was too); and partly because the cousins, or German cousins, or half-German German cousins or whatever they were, resulting from these two cross-over marriages, had complicated things even further by marrying in their turn yet other cousins from the neighbouring branches, so that several of today's members belonged, not to one of the original groups, but to two, in some cases three. The tree bent in on itself, so to speak, its branches merged and twined and intertwined until sorting became, or so Irene feared, the task of a lifetime.

With the branch she found herself attached to, though, identity problems luckily did not arise. Immeshed and far-reaching though it was when integrated with the rest, the nucleus of the original Edmund group was in fact quite small. One floor down from Irene and Tommaso lived Tommaso's elder sister Silvia with her husband Giorgio and their two tiny children, the younger, Olivia, born just before Irene's wedding. Two floors down, on what was called the *piano nobile*, lived Tommaso's father Renzo, a widower ('Be grateful for small mercies,' as Aunt Frances had grimly commented, 'at least you will have no mother-in-law to contend with'), his youngest son, also called Renzo, or Renzino, allegedly to avoid confusion, and his dead wife's mother – Tommaso's grandmother – Savia. Known by everyone, not only her grandchildren, as Nonna Savia. Five people therefore, seven counting the children, ten counting the maids, and three of them sharing a name, because Silvia's elder child was somewhat perversely also called Renzo, abbreviated to Renzetto in his case. Child's play to memorize, in comparison with what lay in store.

But as yet there was no urgency to fit a name to everyone. The other branches of the family, out of what Irene later discovered was a kind of nostalgic respect for the early days of a marriage – particularly strong on the part of the women who, most of them, had known no privacy before or since – continued to leave her tactfully, at times it felt to her almost over-tactfully, alone. Even her sister-in-law Silvia, on whom she had called once or twice in the hope of striking up a friendship, showed herself reserved in this respect. She had been affectionate, welcoming (as welcoming as you could be with two screaming babies and no nanny), had plonked her offspring in a play-pen regardless and chatted with Irene for as long as the visit had lasted, but she had not returned the call.

Later on, when she had found not only her feet but her head and everything else placed between, Irene was to look back on these first months of her marriage, spent in the flat in Florence, as a dull, opaque, somewhat stultifying period. A stretch of quarantine, almost a hiatus between two different lives. While it lasted, however, her new situation contented her well enough, in fact soothed her by its very emptiness. After all, she had married from inertia, from a desire to find a niche for herself where she would be out of everybody's way, and this, it seemed, was what she had found. No complaints therefore. As Aunt Frances said over the telephone when Irene rang her in quest of company (translating the saying from the Italian, because the English version about making your bed and lying in it evidently sounded too *risqué* in the circumstances): 'You wanted a bicycle, didn't you? Then pedal!'

The English saying would have been more appropriate, however, because more than a cyclist's Irene's days seemed to her to pass like those of a courtesan. Tommaso's family had turned out to be much richer than either she or her aunt had supposed, owners not of one chemist's shop but four, plus a recently established pharmaceutical plant in Prato where Tommaso and his father spent most of their time. On her marriage, quite a large inheritance had unexpectedly come to Irene as well from the breaking up of a Trust set up by her grandmother. Money was therefore plentiful all of a sudden, almost too plentiful for comfort. She had a maid who came in in the mornings to do the cleaning and shopping and cooking; she had another who came in in the afternoons to do the washing and ironing; if anything broke or needed fixing she had only to mention it to the *portiere* downstairs and he would be on her doorstep in a trice, pliers or hammer in hand, ready to do her bidding. All this was very nice, very restful, and the *portiere* in particular was good company, but it left Irene with very little to do save to attend to her own person.

In a way this was all she was allowed to do, certainly all she was encouraged to do: her efforts to employ herself, in the kitchen, on the terrace, around the house, were interpreted by her three helpers as criticism of their own work and caused such offence that she was obliged to stop on the spot and let them take command. Tommaso, too, with whom she still had language problems, or at any rate problems of understanding, urged her in the same direction. In him it was predictable, of course, he was obsessed by her body, couldn't stop staring at it, touching it, reaching out for it like a drowning man grabbing at an oar, so its maintenance must have seemed to him a matter of some importance; but even so Irene always found something faintly dispiriting in the counsels he invariably gave her. 'Go to the hairdresser's.' 'Go to the via Tornabuoini and buy a new nightdress.' 'See the *modista* about a hat.' 'Have your legs waxed.' 'Call in a masseuse.' She did all these things because they appeared to be required of her, but she could not say she did them with much inner conviction.

If her days left her with this slightly cloying, slightly meretricious taste in her mouth, the nights, for which the days were nothing but preparation, should have done the same and to a far greater degree. For some reason, though, this was not so. In fact those long explorative hours which she spent under, over or alongside Tommaso's sweat-drenched and apparently tireless body were the only ones that gave her a sense of purpose, of dignity almost. Whatever the frailty of their relationship, born on her side from a lassitude very close to despair, and on his (or so she had begun to suspect) from the intoxication of sex outside the confines of a brothel, this particular foundation stone seemed to hold good. She knew little about this tall, clean, possibly rather conventional young man she had linked her destiny to; conversation with him was difficult – for various reasons, not least the fact that his obsession with her body appeared to make him totally deaf to what she said – and apart from clothes, and to some extent food, she did not know his tastes or his views or his ideas or his ideals or even if he had any. Sometimes, when they had been parted for any length of time, she would have actual difficulty remembering what he looked like, and would find herself, in a mixture of embarrassment and panic, jostling with his features in her mind as if with the pieces of a jigsaw puzzle, trying to make them fit into a whole: brown spaniel eyes, long eyelashes, straight nose; thick eyebrows, slightly too close-set and hairy in the middle; lean cheeks, cleft chin, beard-stubble always in ambush. It never really worked. And yet all the doubts and misgivings on this account that built up during the long uneventful days would disperse as if by magic during the nights, when their bodies joined, and she would find herself clinging to him with a sense of rightness and security, all the more surprising in the context of life-or-death struggle in which their lovemaking was regularly carried out.

The rest of the time, with no body to cling to, she clung to the memory of this certainty. I have not made a mistake after all, she told herself – in the bath, in the streets, in the shops, the gardens, the museums, or wherever her search for occupation took her. I have been rash, I have been weak, I have been careless and bumbling and apathetic, but I have not made a mistake: like a sleepwalker on a precipice, and with just a little merit, I have blindly but unerringly stepped on to firm ground. Mostly she believed this, but sometimes – particularly in the late-afternoons when the batteries of the certainty were running low and the jigsaw of Tommaso's face refused to interlock – she did not.

CHAPTER IV

Whether in fact her peace of mind would have lasted long in this strange, isolated, *demi-mondaine* condition, Irene was never obliged to discover, because with the coming of the warm weather the entire family, herself unquestioningly in its midst, moved to its summer residence in Forte dei Marmi and a totally new life began for her.

When she telephoned to say goodbye Aunt Frances received the news of her departure with a grunt. Even now that she had learnt of their comparative wealth and 'laboratory' chemist status, the doings of the family her niece had married into did not interest her – an attitude which Irene, far from offensive, found pleasantly coherent. 'So you are being turned out to grass with all the other mares, are you?' Aunt Frances said. 'Huh! Typical. And I suppose your husband will stay behind to work and visit you on Sundays, the way they all do? I thought as much. Well, quite a civilized arrangement, I suppose, if you can stick the tedium. Personally I think it would drive me bonkers.'

For the length of the journey and some twenty minutes beyond, in fact until the spaciousness of the new living arrangements was made clear to her, these last words of her aunt's continued to echo menacingly in Irene's ears. The departure from Florence was much as she imagined the sailing of the Ark must have been, when the first raindrops had already begun to fall. First a fleet of taxis was called to accompany to the station those people and objects that were either too large or too frail or too queasy to make the journey by car: Aunts Pussi and Lise with one daughter-in-law and six maids, the hampers containing the bed linen, several bicycles, several dog-baskets, one dog, the teenage Renzino (who was also sick on trains, but *pazienza*, as everyone said, he had to travel somehow), a special anti-asthma mattress, a crate of books belonging to Uncle Otto, a pram and a play-pen and a push-chair belonging to Silvia, or Silvia's children, somebody's fishing tackle, and what seemed to be an unending number of trunks and suitcases. This however was only by way of hors-d'oeuvre or antipasto, and as soon as the taxis were safely on their way, the loading of the four family cars began in earnest; each vehicle by the end of it packed so tightly with people and pets and possessions that the last entrant, usually a child or a dog, had to be passed through the window and then held fast by someone else until the window was rolled up. Both phases of the removal work were carried out in a state of utmost agitation on the part of everybody concerned, save for the teenage Renzino who disdainfully donned a pair of sunglasses and slumped in the back of the taxi feigning sleep. His hope, he confided touchingly to Irene later, being that no one in the neighbourhood would recognize him.

Irene found herself allotted to the 'Tita' family car, wedged in what was evidently intended as a position of great honour between Aunt Tita herself and Aunt Tita's allergy-ridden terrier, Blacky - or 'Blecky' as his owner pronounced it, in an effort to give what she thought maximum Englishness to the vowel. The car suffered two punctures *en route*, Blacky suffered an epileptic fit and had to be doused with mineral water, Irene suffered the embarrassment of having to converse in English with her neighbour throughout without understanding a word of what was said to her, and it was therefore not until their destination had been reached, and the cars had been unloaded and the settling in of the clan members was well under way, that she had been able finally to put Aunt Frances's disturbing parting words from her mind.

Once she had explored her new living-quarters, however, she knew, again with that instinctive certainty she experienced in her marriage bed, that far from driving her bonkers the place was destined to enchant her. The villas owned by the family were three, built amongst a scattering of others in a slightly irregular row on a strip of land between beach and pine wood, about, Irene judged, four or five minutes' walk from the town. (In fact it turned out to be six, seven if you had a pram to push, and two and a half on a bicycle.) There was the original villa, Edmund's, in which Tommaso's close family and Irene herself were to live – a squat, white, serious-looking building which made no concessions to its seaside environment; there was Pussi's villa, built by her next door to her brother's at the time of her marriage in almost identical style, although with one or two more modern features such as french windows and a sun-terrace; and third in the row, far grander and newer than the others (and also, in Irene's opinion, far grimmer, being of marble inside and out and tightly hemmed in by cedar trees, planted full grown at great expense) there was Tita's villa, specially designed for her by her rich and indulgent husband shortly before his death a mere fifteen years back. Irene's opinion was not shared by the rest of the family, though, who, one and all, considered the building magnificent and a showpiece.

Aunt Lise, having married less advantageously than her sisters, had no villa of her own; but her summer separation from the rest of the family being unthinkable, an arrangement had been made by which she and Uncle Otto and their contingent rented the ground floor of Pussi's villa while Pussi's contingent retired, with varying degrees of good to middling grace, to the upper storeys. This, however, it took Irene quite some time to understand: to begin with, when she saw all the coming and going through the front entrance and all the mattress-beating and the blanket-shaking that went on as if in preparation for a billeting regiment, it merely seemed to invalidate the mapping out of the family structure she had done thus far.

The three villas, though separate, formed a kind of loose unity, having connecting gates (opened on arrival and never afterwards closed) leading from garden to garden, through which all the inhabitants – dogs, children, nursemaids, parents – wandered more or less at will, apart from a few time restrictions relating to the afternoon rest-hour. There was only one telephone too, situated in the hall of the first villa, the one Tommaso's family and Irene herself lived in, which everyone, domestics included, made use of through a complicated appointment system involving much lingering around and smoking and coffee drinking while waiting for the instrument to ring. And although each villa had its own facilities for this purpose, for some reason or other – most likely habit, Irene decided, or else a desire for companionship on the part of the washers – anything connected with laundering was also done in the precincts of the first villa, in a remote area of the garden known as *la Fontana*, the fountain: a scrubby quadrangle of herbs and fig trees and washtubs and clotheslines which held an almost magical appeal for all living creatures from lizards upwards. So to some extent Aunt Frances was right, Irene realized, as day by day the layout and the customs of the place became more familiar to her: the Family, with a capital 'F', was all about her and made its presence felt.

She also realized that her aunt had been apt in her metaphor of the mares and the grass. None of the gardens, not even Tita's where every effort had been made to cultivate a proper *prato all'Inglese*, boasted a blade of grass, but nevertheless the constant, gentle rhythm of the life in the three villas which established itself as soon as the flurry of arrival was over, not to mention the absence during the weekdays of all adult males save for Uncle Otto and the gardener, did indeed, Irene found, give you the impression you were part of a privileged herd of livestock put out to grass.

As with the ordering of the branches of the family tree, it was the elder members who implicitly dictated this rhythm. Not because they were authoritative or bossy, but, quite the opposite, because the quiet contented buzz of their presence created a kind of background music to which everyone, even the children, felt unconsciously bound to keep time. In the mornings the four households would go about their separate business, breakfasting, shopping, organizing their meals for the day. Organizing also their *toilettes*, because, even for Uncle Otto who relished shocking his wife and sisters-in-law by his deliberate shabbiness, dressing was vitally important. There would be a brief pre-lunch gathering of the aunts round about midday under Tita's foreboding trees, in which those maids who had no last-minute frying or pasta-boiling to do could participate, and then everyone would disappear again into the cool of the houses. To emerge in the garden of the main villa on the dot of five, dolled up to the nines, chairs in tow and knitting in hand, ready to take part in what was called – only semi-accurately, for the term was intended as a beverage reference, not a time reference – the 'five o'clock'.

This event was the high-point of the day, and not only for the inhabitants of the three villas. A little confusingly from Irene's point of view, who had just begun to feel she was getting somewhere with her name-tags, these gatherings were regularly attended by a dozen or so neighbours, plus children, plus *tatas* or nursemaids, swelling the ranks of those to be recognized and greeted when encountered by at least a score (for fortunately Irene did not think she need bother too much about the children). More confusing still, several of these people bore German surnames and behaved with the intimacy of relatives, being part of a small original colony who had followed the example of Edmund and his sisters and had bought pieces of coastland cheaply, in the days when Italians still shunned the sun. Most of them, as far as Irene was able to make out, seemed to be watchmakers or printers or coin dealers; and all of them, despite their surnames and the Mittel-European flavour of their trades, seemed to be by now completely Italian.

Tea, or 'five o'clock', was served until eight o'clock, being passed round the circle on a trolley which seemed to move forward from chair to chair on its own accord. Invitations to supper were never extended, not even between branches, and punctually, with the removal of the trolley, Nonna Savia and the aunts would take leave of their guests and of one another and disappear inside again, signalling the moment for the evening meal. Only if the night were very hot would they reassemble outside afterwards. Otherwise, by the same unspoken rule that governed the laundering and the 'five o'clock', they would gather inside the hall of the first villa, where they would sit for hours in great discomfort, perching upon the hard wooden benches amidst oars and beach balls and fishing tackle, in close proximity to the telephone, and gossip for as long as the fancy took them.

Irene wondered what her aunt would have thought, could she have seen her adapting to this rhythm without a murmur, indeed with positive enjoyment? Most likely she would have thought, Poor Irene, they've made a proper little bourgeoise out of her and no mistake. And said it too, only she would probably have used the term *Hausfrau*, not bourgeoise, to convey double disapproval. The afternoon circle would doubtless have been the target of her particular scorn: 'Just look at all those old trouts with their teacups and their knitting! How *can* you, Irene? And your mother who so wanted you to marry a diplomat and lead a glittering life!' Or some similar reproach, Irene could just hear her making it.

But, apart from the fact that her freedom within the family was absolute and she was under no obligation to join in anything unless she wanted to, the more accustomed she grew to her new surroundings, the less Aunt Frances's opinions seemed to matter to Irene. She knew, even without the signpost of the knitting circle, that her marriage had not introduced her into glittering nor even faintly shining company in the way her aunt intended (perhaps she would have preferred for her niece a breeder of golden cocker spaniels?), but she knew she was among friends, among people who wished her well and who accepted her, warmly and uncritically, as one of themselves. It was her first taste, really, of belonging somewhere and she could not help but relish it.

All the more so since the somewhere, sandwiched as it was between sea the colour of turquoise and mountains so high that their winter snow had not yet melted, was not only consoling and friendly territory but also very beautiful. Each day Irene would wake to the smell of coffee boiling in the kitchen and the sounds of Silvia ministering to her babies, and would cross over to the window and open the shutters and stand there for some moments, almost in disbelief that it could be so beautiful, the air so fragrant, the sun so dependable. During these moments the residue of doubt she still occasionally felt about the wisdom of her choice – or lack of choice – would dissipate almost entirely: even if things do not work out, she thought (meaning by things her life, her future, above all her marriage), it will still be here, in this setting, that I will be called upon to face the consequences. And in this setting, with the sun, this skyline, this house and these people and the sense of peace that they infuse in me, everything will be bearable. Even boredom and dissatisfaction. Even downright unhappiness, should it ever come.

CHAPTER V

As things turned out, unhappiness took a long time coming, and when it came it wore a strange disguise. For three summers running Irene accompanied the family in its seasonal movements, becoming more and more integrated, more and more part of the tribe. A year after her marriage her first child was born, a boy. She called him Giotto, after the Tuscan painter, in an effort to please everyone, even Aunt Frances.

Any lingering reserves that members of the family might have had on her account – any regrets for the missing trousseau, any censure for the capers in the car – dissolved permanently with this event. The menfolk were still more gallant towards her, the womenfolk, young and old, still more adoring. Uncle Otto composed an atrocious poem about the *Bell'Inglesotto di nome Giotto*, Aunt Tita as an unheard of favour (she was known to have said of her own sons, Guido and the thin but voracious Marco, that she would have mothered them more willingly had they been puppies) offered to babysit whenever Irene wanted, Nonna Savia made her a baptism present of her best pearls. Everyone – from the youngest of the children to the oldest and trickiest of the adults – went out of their way to please her and to show her they were pleased by her. Silvia, in particular, who for the first summer had continued to use her affability like a kind of fence beyond which Irene had been unable to penetrate, dismantled the fence and became like a sister to her, offering a friendship of an intensity and quality Irene had not thought possible, never having had a friend of her own age before.

They were closer than sisters really. Like Siamese twins joined at head and heart, they became inseparable. United not so much by motherhood as by the desire to rid themselves now and again of motherhood and its cares, they liaised, supported one another, connived, plotted and confessed, until there was nothing they did not know about each other, nothing – no fear, no taste, no judgement – they did not share. Irene, on Tommaso's insistence, had a nurse for Giotto: she bypassed the nurse and took on most of the work herself, so as not to lose contact with Silvia. Silvia, on Giorgio's insistence, was supposed, vice versa, to do everything for the children herself, it was part of his theory on childcare: she defied him and delegated when she could, so as to make time for Irene.

In the winters, in Florence, they saw each other every day. Resentful almost of the masonry that separated them, they would trudge up and down the stairs, cradles and push-chairs in tow, and set up camp together in whichever apartment seemed more convenient. Usually Irene's, where the nurse – young and uncomplaining – could be used for triple baby-parking, giving Silvia and Irene a chance to go shopping for clothes or get their hair done, or just talk to one another without the interference of screams. They would not separate until nightfall, when the children's bedtime and Tommaso's return from work made it imperative, and even then would often leave one of the husbands to babysit alone, and meet up again after supper. In the summer, with no structural divides to get in the way, they lived in virtual symbiosis, establishing their own ménage within the ménage: going early to the beach, coming back early, eating with the children at their own times, and spending every moment of their free time together on the roof of the villa, where they would lie for hours, stark naked, with the ladder of access drawn up, smoking and talking and cultivating their suntan, all with rapturous earnestness. For the first time in her life (because Giotto was perfect but he was too small and too much part of her to count) Irene found herself totally in sympathy, in unison, in harmony with another human being. It was a wonderful feeling. Like being in love, she presumed, only without the tension: for even if the romance should cool, she knew that neither she nor Silvia could ever cut the ties that bound them, ever move away. They were saddled with one another, and the saddles fitted and they wore them like an indispensable part of their everyday dress.

Everybody in the family, or nearly everybody, approved of this closeness: the rearing of babies drew young women naturally together, it was felt, and left husbands equally naturally in the cold. Nonna Savia and Aunt Lise had been thick as thieves in their time – still were for that matter – and had very properly stood for no meddling in their affairs from Edmund and Otto; Tita's two daughters-in-law, Eva and Carla, who had given birth within a month of each other, had actually sent their husbands back to Mamma for a year and set up house together. Men who wanted their wives to themselves should think twice before they had children, and if they didn't then it was their own lookout.

Tommaso, brought up in this conviction, respecting these priorities, formulated no complaints, not even to himself, but Irene could sometimes sense in him a kind of baffled jealousy. His sexual demands on her increased, became at times inopportune; he would catch hold of her as she was leaving the flat on her way to Silvia's, corner her as she and Silvia spoke together on the telephone, rub himself against her and moan his urgency into her ear as if challenging her to choose between them: sister or brother, talk or action. At times it was exciting, as he intended it to be; at times, Irene found, it was simply a delay and a nuisance. If he could have given her, not all but even a quarter, a fraction of what Silvia gave her – in the way of companionship, of fun, of understanding things without having to spell them out letter by letter – then perhaps, who knows, she would have spent her time just as willingly with him. But apart from the physical bond which had seemed so promising, so reassuring in the early days of their marriage and now, on the contrary, was beginning to seem so restrictive, Tommaso appeared to have nothing to offer. Or not, at any rate, in the way of entertainment.

He was interested in his work, but he thought, quite rightly, that Irene would not be. He was interested in his son, but only to the extent of Giotto's physical health which was fortunately so robust as to pre-empt enquiry. He retained a certain, although dwindling, interest in clothes, Irene's and his, in this order. He followed football and motor-racing on the radio – not cycling because Aunt Pussi had taught him as a child it was plebeian. While it was airborne he followed the flight of the Zeppelin; while this other monument of the modern world was precipitating he followed the crash of the Wall Street Stock Exchange. Otherwise the radius of his attention seemed still, a full three years after marriage, to encompass Irene's body and nothing but Irene's body, and a fairly restricted part of it at that. Recently, but only very recently, books of a tamely political cast had begun to appear on his bedside table – Gentile, Ojetti, Mussolini's collected speeches – but Irene had never seen him reading one: he merely used them as a prop for the crossword puzzle he doodled with while waiting for her to come to bed. All in all their relationship continued to be comfortable but curiously empty: from strangeness to one another they seemed to have passed to familiarity, with no learning process in between, no moments of discovery. Perhaps, Irene thought without the idea greatly troubling her, because apart from his good looks and his good nature there was nothing much in Tommaso to discover.

Silvia's case was slightly different. Her husband, Giorgio, also resented the friendship between his wife and Irene, but unlike Tommaso he had no difficulty in making his resentment explicit. Either to himself or to anyone else. He called them unabashedly *le lesbicone*, puzzling the aunts and Nonna Savia who either didn't know the word or didn't know how it was intended. Baptized an 'intellectual' by the family, who otherwise did not know how to account for his apparently interminable student career, he sneered openly at what he considered the frivolous foundations of their friendship. 'Discussing *The Critique of Pure Reason*?' he would ask, when he came back from the university to find them cutting out patterns for beach pyjamas or experimenting with face-packs or hair-dyes. 'Giving yourselves up to speculative thought?' And with a groan he would throw himself on the sofa where he spent most of his time when at home. '*Dio mio*! Doesn't anything ever enter your chicken-sized heads except peroxide fumes? Don't you know what those louts have just done to Toscanini? Does the name Gandhi mean nothing to you? *Dio Cristo*! When will you wake up to what the real world is about?'

But since this was the very question that Irene and Silvia would often ask themselves about him – wondering when he would stop living off Silvia's money, start earning some of his own, start treating the children as something more than play-things, start growing *up*, for goodness sake – their response was usually a yawn, followed by swifter snipping or more dedicated daubing. Giorgio read everything, followed everything, had theories about everything from breast-feeding to knot-tying to constitutional government, but did, from the point of view of work or study or even practical help around the house, virtually nothing. His habit of delivering *ex cathedra* pronouncements (or *ex* sofa pronouncements, because that was invariably where he made them from), while it may have captivated Silvia in the early days of courtship, had already begun to pall on her when Irene first met her, and now exasperated her beyond reaction.

Giorgio, Irene could tell, blamed her, not Silvia, for this gradual falling off of wifely admiration; saw her as a suffragette, a trouble-maker, and did everything he could to get the rest of the family to see likewise. But Irene being by now much more part of the clan than he was, he could gain no support for this view, not even from Tommaso who should have been his natural ally. The two brothers-in-law, one so upright, one almost constantly horizontal, one with a thousand interests, one with scarcely any, mistrusted one another almost on principle, and it was sufficient for one to entertain an opinion for the other to diverge from it. Not declaredly, that would have been to pay the other too great a compliment, but silently, by refusing to consider it or even acknowledge it had been expressed.

Opposition to the friendship-cum-love affair between Silvia and Irene was therefore scant and divided, and what little there was only added zest to it. It was fun to thwart Tommaso now and then of his conjugal rights, it made his reactions less predictable; it was even more fun to give Giorgio the slip and leave him spouting out his judgements on the National

Socialist Party and the Chinese–Japanese War to an empty room. It introduced that note of wickedness, or shared and justified blame, that seemed to Irene to be an essential cementing ingredient of their friendship – perhaps of any friendship.

It was with a sense of almost perfect happiness, then, that in the middle of May 1932, well ahead of schedule, and well ahead of the others who had a multiple first-communion party of the younger members of the clan to attend, Irene made her fourth journey to the villa in Forte dei Marmi for her fourth summer there. She travelled by car with Silvia and they took turns at the wheel, feeling very adult, very dashing (but not, funnily enough, all that daring: it was too early in Italy for the notion to have formed itself that driving was dangerous or unsuitable for women, people just had no opinion on the matter at all). Until the rest of the family joined them they were to be allowed to keep the car for their own use: Irene was expecting a second child in September and it was decided she and Silvia had better be mobile, just in case; it would not do for her to fall into the hands of the local doctor – notoriously grubby and stained with Tuscan cigar smoke. In the back sat the three children, the young nursemaid Carmela, and Assunta, who had claimed at the last moment, undisputed, that they could not do without her: a perfect group to Irene's way of thinking, impossible to improve on.

The trio of villas was not entirely empty when they arrived. Uncle Otto and Aunt Lise, defying custom for once, and defying also the agitated wrath of their sons- and daughters-in-law who declared they would worry themselves sick thinking what terrible accidents might happen to the two elderly people alone, had for the first time since their children were of school-age spent the whole winter there. From the fervour with which they greeted the arrival of the car and its occupants, it seemed their experiment in tardy independence had not been a total success.

They had been busy, though – perhaps to counteract their melancholy, or else simply to keep themselves warm, for none of the villas was centrally heated. Uncle Otto had done a lot of gardening in all three gardens, and Aunt Lise, having been left the keys to the first villa for purposes of telephoning, had not only dusted the house regularly herself but the moment she had heard they were coming had called in a team of spring-cleaners from the town to make everything ready for Silvia's and Irene's arrival. Assunta, prowling round the kitchen in fierce concentration, divining for dirt, said it was money thrown out of the window and you couldn't tell anybody had done any work at all, but Irene, who normally found the opening up of the house a rather depressing affair, was delighted. She was particularly relieved not to be confronted by the annual drama of the sparrows which regularly nested in the windows between panes and shutters during the family's absence, and equally regularly had to be dislodged, creating all sorts of domestic conflicts: the maids who wanted to be rid of the fledglings, the children who wanted to save them, and she and Silvia who knew you couldn't save them and that it was kinder not to, but who none the less allowed themselves to be persuaded, time after melancholy time, into trying. There'd be no trafficking with shoeboxes and cotton wool and insects on the end of toothpicks this year, thank goodness, and no pathetic little stick-boned funerals either, the cleaners from the town had seen to that.

She went to her bedroom and lay down on the bed, brandishing Giotto above her in a kind of drunkenness of content. Life was good, she decided, life was almost perfect. Aunt Frances could say what she liked about mares and foals and domesticity and getting stuck in a rut, but she loved this rut she was stuck in, and she loved the herd she was part of and she loved the grazing ground. She loved her foals too, the finished one (at this point she lowered Giotto and began freeing him of his town clothes so that he should share her holiday feeling) and the one in the making. Considerate of it to wait until September: like that she had all the summer before her, or almost. The bicycle outings to Viareggio might be off – she didn't think she could keep her balance on a bike the shape she was now – but everything else would be just the same and better. There would be the sea and the sun and the swimming; the picnics on the beach, when Assunta and the other maids marched down from the villa in triumphant procession with baskets from which they extracted, like magicians, tablecloths and cutlery and a fully cooked three-course meal ('We're not having word go round that our family eats bread and *salame*, *nossignore*!'). There would be the ice-cream-and-*bomboloni* orgies along the seafront in the afternoon; the expeditions to the jetty to watch the unloading of the marble-boats and to cheer the great teams of oxen with their plaited tails and gold-tipped horns as they drew the blocks away; the trips to the mountains to eat rye bread and home-cured ham; the cinema evenings when everyone took chairs and cushions and sat in the improvised open-air theatre eating pumpkin seeds and hissing at the operator each time the reel ran out, or the film snapped, or a lizard parked itself on the sheet that acted as screen and did something disrespectful like crawl up Mussolini's nose or down the leading lady's *décolletage*. There would be all this, and Silvia in the room right next door to share it with, and Tommaso and Giorgio – for a while anyway: university terms were brief in Italy and Giorgio was in fact threatening to arrive fairly soon – safely in Florence, a hundred kilometres away, and *without*, what was more, the use of a car. It was a moment of satisfaction so intense, a feeling so smug, so secure, that had Irene been at all superstitious she must have suspected a price to be paid – a tribute to the gods who, so Uncle Otto had once told her in utmost seriousness, did not like the sound of human gloating and always intervened to stop it. But such thoughts were foreign to her in all senses. Nor when the tax came, as it did promptly, less than a minute later, did she recognize it as such: for a while it merely seemed another bonus, another of the summer's enticements.

Still heady with happiness, she got up off the bed, deposited Giotto, naked and shoeless. on the floor, promising him they would go to the beach with the others the moment the unpacking was finished, and sent him toddling off to Carmela to find a bathing suit. Then she crossed over to the window, and with another silent murmur of thanks to the cleaners, threw open the window to survey her beloved summer kingdom.

It was all there, richer and denser even than she remembered:

the clear blue sky still unstained by sunset, the swifts diving across it, the soft lapping noise of the sea, the smell of resin wafting from the pines, the great bank of bougainvillaea on the wall that divided the garden from that of the next-door villa just coming into colour. Uncle Otto had got the chairs out already, as if in readiness for the knitting circle which he affected so to despise. The only difference, so far as Irene could see, was that the next-door villa, which for the past three summers had stood empty (provoking much speculation from the aunts: What could have happened to the Lessings? Had the Ammiraglio been stationed abroad? Was his wife expecting yet another child? Had they gone and bought a better house somewhere else, the traitors?), was now open and lived in. On the terrace, which Irene could look across to on almost equal terms, so high did it stand, amidst an array of towels and dripping bathing suits which from the looks of it he had just that minute finished hanging, stood a young man in a white beach robe, holding a tiny child by the hand. The eldest and youngest, presumably, of the large Lessing brood: Assunta always said – not entirely approvingly – that everyone in that family had to help out with the chores, even the males.

The hood of the young man's robe was up, leaving the face in partial shadow, but nevertheless Irene could tell that he was startlingly beautiful. (Perhaps even unsuitably beautiful for someone of his background: hadn't Aunt Pussi said something about him studying law? How could anyone hope to be taken seriously as a lawyer, she wondered, with a face like that?) He was staring straight at her, with a steadiness that she knew instinctively she must interrupt if it were not to prove an embarrassment to both of them later, when, as they were bound to do sooner or later, they met on a social basis.

Options flitted through her mind: a neighbourly wave? A smile? A dignified '*Buonasera*', as befitted a young woman in her condition, and then a closing of the shutters? But as if hypnotized she let them flit, and returned the stare, gazing back solemnly at the unknown face with exactly the same unflinching, unleavened earnestness. Fully aware of the implications which built up, second by second, like numbers squared and resquared, becoming just as quickly unmanageable. Thou shalt not stare, not like that at any rate, not that hard, not that long.

Although how long in actual fact the moment lasted Irene wasn't sure. Afterwards, bundling Giotto into his bathing suit, who at some point had come back into the bedroom with it dangling from his hand, asking for her assistance, she tried to persuade herself that it could only have been a few seconds – a harmless length of time anyway, far too short for anything irreparable to have taken place. But even as she thought this with one part of her mind, another, deeper-set part, which seemed only now to have found a voice, told her that time as measured by the clock didn't come into it and that the irreparable had already happened.

Feeling suddenly very energetic, and with a speed that she would later come to recognize as a strategic way of leaving her conscience in the lurch (or her sense of dignity, or sense of ridicule, or whichever the particular opponent was that needed foiling), Irene swung Giotto into his favourite position astride her stomach and went into Silvia's room to collect the other two children. 'You go ahead with the unpacking if you want to,' she told Silvia, bustling Renzetto and Olivia out of the door and hardly waiting for an answer. 'We're off to the beach before it gets too late.'

Once outside in the garden she no longer had the commanding view over the terrace she had had from her bedroom, and for a moment she was tempted to raise her head quite deliberately to see if the young man was still there, watching, tarrying, not comprehending. However, she resisted the urge. If the look they had exchanged had meant anything, she thought fleetingly as she grabbed Renzetto by the hand – 'No, we can't take the beach ball, we'll take it tomorrow. No, leave that too, come *on*, *vieni*, *vieni*!' – he would *know* what she was doing, and know exactly what to do himself. It was by way of being a test, although a test of what, she didn't really know. Of his similarity to her, she supposed, of the strength or weakness of the fellow-feeling between them. The essential thing, anyway, was speed: it wouldn't count if he followed, it would only count if he twigged and did the same thing at the same time.

She walked fast down the path, still carrying Giotto, who was an even slower walker than the other two, and opened the gate that led to the beach. For a moment her heart sank, or rather sobered itself to adjust to disappointment. Then it rose again in a great giddy leap. He was there. Young Master Lessing – absurd, but she did not yet know his Christian name – had passed the test with flying colours. He had guessed her intentions and was standing on the other side of the footpath waiting for her; waiting to precede or follow her to the beach. Well! What do you know! Snap and Snap-pool! Her amusement was so great she wanted to laugh out loud.

The young man, however, when Irene plucked up her courage to look him in the eye from this closer and far more compromising distance, did not seem to share her high spirits. He returned the look, openly, unabashedly, with the same penetrating intensity as before, but this time there was something harder in his expression. No, not harder, sadder. Definitely sadder.

The smile on Irene's lips faded; the jet of her amusement subsided, turned off at source like a tap. What had she done, she asked herself anxiously, in this brief space of time, to sadden him? Had he changed his mind about her? Had he made a mistake? Didn't he like the look of her at close range? Then she saw him, briefly, almost shiftily, lower his gaze towards her stomach and back again, and realized what it was that was troubling him. The window, of course: from the window he had not seen her stomach, and not seen Giotto either. Perhaps judging by her top-half alone, he had thought she was just an ordinary available young woman – a guest or a cousin or a maid, at the worst someone's girlfriend or fiancée on a visit. Whereas now there was no doubt about who or what she was: a wife and mother and heavily pregnant on top of it. Also a shameless flirt. No wonder, she thought, growing suddenly sad herself, no wonder he didn't like the look of her at close range, who would?

It was impossible now to disappoint the children by going

back: she had promised them a paddle, maybe even a bathe if the water wasn't too cold. With a gesture she hoped was suitable for a snubbed matron – something between a worldly shrug and a penitent smile – she turned away from the young man and without a backward glance walked towards the beach. Talking very loudly and animatedly to the children, to cover the smart she felt inside.

The sea was beautiful, so clear at the edge it looked like drinking water. The three children splashed around, half in, half out, while Irene waded out a little further and put her arms and forehead in the water. She wished now she had changed into a bathing suit herself, a swim would have cleared her head for her, cooled down her temperature which now seemed to be running at a hundred and five. When she turned to wade back, though, she saw another figure on the beach, standing alone a little further down, looking hard in her direction, and realized that the young man had followed her – undaunted, evidently, by her bulk and married status.

Once again, with the same switchback rapidity, her mood changed, her spirits rocketed. It already seemed to her unwise to make signs in front of the children, but she thought if she did not smile at this point she would burst. So she smiled, the widest and friendliest smile she could muster, spreading her hands wide as well, as much as to say: I am sorry, this is the situation. What is to be done about it?

The young man smiled back, showing his teeth for the first time. The front incisor was darker than the others: a blemish which Irene registered with a shock as familiar to her. Perhaps (although she knew she hadn't) she had been told about it or had seen a photograph. Then with a timeless, dramatic gesture (like Christ, she thought: white-robed, by the sea, doing solemn things with no fear of looking foolish), he stretched out his arms to her, the hands, like hers, held a little wide.

He kept the pose for some moments, long enough to make sure it had been well observed, then turned away and ran back to the villas, leaping over the sand in gigantic bounds as if the meeting had had an invigorating effect on him as well.

What the gesture meant exactly, Irene did not know: it could have meant Come, it could have meant Go, it could have meant Too bad and what a shame we didn't meet earlier, or simply, What a mess, but she thought about it at length that night before she fell asleep. Carefully, one could almost say practisedly had not the situation been entirely new to her, she refrained from thinking of very much else.

CHAPTER VI

By the simple method of not having them, Irene continued to keep her mind free of any troublesome thoughts for several weeks. There was no smothering involved, no chasing the thoughts away or blocking them on the threshold of consciousness, they simply did not find their way into her head at all.

She acted, and this was presently enough. The days, from long and lazy with plenty of time for sunbathing on the roof with Silvia and smoking and talking and reading and nail-varnishing and tweezing out hairs from unwanted places one by one, suddenly became short and full of things to do. The roof was out for other reasons as well: a person could neither see nor be seen from it, and seeing was vital, indeed you could say that it was everything, a day without a sighting was a day wasted, a day lost.

Things had to be done in order to make room for other things; certain things had to be done much faster than formerly in order to make room for certain other things that now had to be done much more slowly. Washing the children, feeding them, dressing them, putting them to bed, were time-wasters and the quicker they were over and done with the better; getting Giotto off to sleep, on the other hand, when Irene could stand by the bedroom window, reading, telling stories, in full view of the terrace below, was something to be protracted for as long as possible. He might be there. He often was there, he was beginning to learn her timetable. As a general rule, she found, anything that entailed being outside in the garden (and particularly mobile things like teaching Renzetto to ride a bicycle, or helping Assunta hang the washing in the Fontana, which with a bit of careful manoeuvring could bring her very close to her target indeed) called for slow, drawn-out motions; anything that kept her indoors, without plausible access to the window, called for speed. The short journey to the beach, which at present was the only moment of the day in which she could hope to see her young neighbour at close range without the wall or the branches of bougainvillaea in between, had to be undertaken with *extreme* slowness, and repeated as often as could be contrived without arousing Silvia's suspicions. Irene became adept at forgetting essential things like water and towels and sunglasses and at heaving herself up from the sand with a fine show of reluctance to go and fetch them, 'No, no, nobody move. My own stupid fault. Walking is good for me anyway, I'll go, *vado io.*' Whereas the actual stay at the beach, where each family of residents had for decades occupied its own traditional patch, hundreds of polite metres distant from the next, had to be shortened: there was no satisfaction to be gained from staring at a small figure on the horizon or a pinpoint of a head bobbing in the sea, which when it drew near usually belonged to the wrong person anyway.

In fact, although Irene was seldom calm enough or aware enough during this first hectic phase of the romance to realize it, there was no satisfaction to be had in almost anything any more. Satisfaction had walked out of the window on that first afternoon when she had opened it and looked out into the terrace across the way. Satisfaction belonged to the past. The present was composed of craving – mindless, instinctive, rat-in-a-labyrinth craving – and of little moments of respite as with the engineering of each new meeting of eyes the craving was temporarily assuaged. She knew his name: Giuliano. She knew, from a hundred signs invisible to anyone but themselves, that whatever it was she felt about him – attraction, desire, curiosity, it was hard to put a name to it – he felt about her; perhaps, judging by his behaviour, which from what little she could see of it was scattier at times than her own, even more strongly. She knew also that things could not go on as they were, that no affair of this intensity could remain indefinitely at the optical stage, and that sooner or later something was bound to happen to bring them closer together; but while desiring this with all her being, she found it at the same time impossible to take any practical step, no matter how small, no matter how halting, to bring it about. Even when their timing was accurate and she and Giuliano met on the seabound path, alone, unobserved, face to yearning face, she couldn't bring herself to stop and speak to him; all she could do was to slow her steps and gaze, and gaze, and gaze. It wasn't that she feared rebuff – things had clearly gone well past the rebuff stage now; it was simply that she felt obscurely that it was better – not morally better, not tactically better, just better – to make no deliberate acceleration of tempo on her own initiative. The situation ought perhaps to have seemed funny to her, a Pyramus and Thisbe farce complete with wall and chink and endless missed appointments, but somehow it never did. To begin with because she was too involved, too trapped in her voyeur's routine to see the funny side of anything; and later – well, later because by the time she was able to see it, *really* see it, with knowledge and objectivity, the funniness had gone, run like a bright colour into the surrounding darker shades.

The only critical faculty, almost the only intellectual faculty that continued to work unimpaired during this phase of otherwise total mindlessness, was cunning. In fact, cunning being until now one of the least used accomplishments in Irene's repertoire, it worked a good deal better. Assunta, standing chattering, sheet in hand, one metre from the wall, while Irene's eyes sent darts of passion to a spot just beyond her shoulder; Carmela, trotting along the road beside her with the children, crossing the trajectory of a look so ardent it should have frazzled her; Aunt Lise and Uncle Otto, sitting guilelessly in the garden while the darts continued to flash to and fro above their heads – none of these people, all of them in close daily contact with her, had any inkling of what was taking place, any suspicion of the truth, of this Irene was sure because she made sure. You did not necessarily have to be a master chess player, she discovered, to play two games at once.

And the same, with even more confidence, could be said about the children, whom she was careful, despite her at times frenzied impatience to be elsewhere, never to overlook, never to shove aside, never to stint of her attention (even though sometimes it was only an oblique, epidermic attention, with the bulk of it going willy-nilly elsewhere). The real test of her cunning, however, was with Silvia. Silvia, her constant companion, her alter ego, the person who knew her better almost than she did herself, was her litmus paper: if Silvia noticed nothing – and again Irene was confident that she *had* so far noticed nothing, or she would surely have remarked on it – then her secret was safe. Time to start worrying when Silvia herself started worrying and asking awkward questions; until then the coast was clear and the two-sided staring match could go on, inebriating and unchecked, and that was all that mattered.

To see, to be seen, to be seen seeing, to see again. *Ad libitum. Ad infinitum.* (Not *ad nauseam*, because of seeing there would never be enough.) The entire world, the entire universe, seemed to consist in nothing but the rotation and alignment of these four small orbs: her eyes and Giuliano's. Everything else – her daily life with Silvia and the children, Tommaso's weekend visits, even the approaching birth of the child she was carrying – was reduced for the time being to the status of planetary dust, of interfering motes. Drastic, possibly shocking if she had had time to stop and think of it, but that was the way it was.

At some moment during this period, Giorgio arrived. In past years Irene had dreaded his arrival almost as much as Silvia did: Giorgio took great and discernible pleasure in upsetting their schedule, reorganizing their menus, stirring up the children and generally sabotaging their peace. Now, save for a perfunctory call to the baker to step up the order of bread, she hardly noticed he was there. If anything his presence was a bonus: it kept Silvia busier and her mind on other things.

Aunt Lise had a nasty fall when picking cherries with Irene in the Fontana. She barely noticed that either, just scooped the old woman up and dusted her down, never allowing her eyes to veer from horizontal, not even to check the damage. How could she afford to look down when Giuliano was there, within three metres, on the other side of the wall, and when she might not see him for the rest of the day?

Giotto pushed a bean up his nostril and it stuck there. This caused Irene a moment's maternal anguish, but the moment the bean was out she spun round in the direction of the terrace, holding the retrieved object triumphantly between thumb and finger; happy for Giotto's release from pain, but happy too to have an excuse to look upwards, beyond the bean, at something quite different.

In absence of moves on either side, false or otherwise, this moonstruck interlude could have lasted indefinitely. Insofar as she was capable of hoping, or indeed of doing anything other than dissemble and stare, stare and dissemble, Irene rather hoped that it would. Like a drug addict's, the range of her pleasure had shrunk but she had no wish to enlarge it. Round about the middle of June, however, confirmations and communions celebrated, school terms over, exams safely passed, the rest of the family arrived. And with its arrival, suddenly, painfully, if only for a brief moment before it clouded over again, Irene's horizon cleared. The haze, trance, thrall, or whatever it was, lifted and she saw herself for what she was, or what she feared she was about to become: a traitor to her kind.

She went to the main gate with Silvia to welcome everyone and help unload the luggage. The scene was the familiar one of summers past: bustle, confusion, excitement, escaping pets heading towards the Fontana, escaping children heading towards the beach, pursued by unheeded shouts from parents and keepers: 'Change into your beach clothes first!' 'Don't get sand in your shoes!' 'Keep out of the water!' 'Don't run!' 'Don't sweat!' Blacky in the aftermath of his annual fit, lying in state on the running board of the largest car, with Aunt Tita kneeling in the road beside him mopping at him with a cologne-drenched handkerchief; Eva and Carla, standing by limply, not daring to do anything until Mamma-in-law's favourite was pronounced out of danger; the other adults scurrying backwards and forwards – they had other things to think of than the nursing of a spoilt hypochondriac dog; Uncle Otto, too old for weights but ashamed to be seen inactive, busily rubbing at the windscreens of the cars with his shirt-tail; the *carozza* driver, Achille, who had ferried the train group from the station, standing by philosophically, watching and grazing his horse in the ditch and waiting for his fare.

Irene saw all this, and for a moment, as she walked-*cum*-waddled down the drive, face smiling, arms outstretched, heart absent, totally elsewhere, she was filled with shame. These are my people, she thought, my family. The only real family I have ever had. They have taken me in, given me a home – two homes, to be exact, and one particularly beautiful one – affection, warmth, an anchorage, security, everything I was lacking before, and this is how I repay them: by playing them false and making sheep's eyes over the garden wall with a total stranger. What can have got into me? What can I have been thinking of? For their sakes (their collective sakes: it was strange, but her falsity towards Tommaso didn't really seem to matter except insofar as he was a member of the group), I must put an end to this foolishness immediately.

It *was* only a moment: as she carried the few light bundles entrusted to her back to the villa, Irene already found herself looking up again in the direction of the terrace, scanning, hoping, with the same unthinking compulsion as before – gape, gape, gape, like a hare in the headlights or a chicken with its beak trained to a white line. But it was a moment that had left its mark. That afternoon, for almost the first time since they had been there, she left Giotto to play with his cousins in Carmela's care and kept her tryst with Silvia on the rooftop.

Silvia was pleased to see her although a little puzzled. 'But I thought you couldn't manage the ladder any more?' she said with a slightly accusatory note in her voice, wriggling snakewise across the platform to help haul Irene to safety.

Was that, then, the excuse she had put forward? Irene supposed that it must have been. She shrugged. 'Well I can,' she replied, 'or I wouldn't be here. Only I don't always feel like it. And besides, too much sun is bad for my stomach now that it's getting so taut. It's got some funny brown marks on it already.'

'*Balle*,' said Silvia, her favourite fast new word for nonsense. 'The more sun the better. It'll stay flabby for ages if you keep it covered. White and flabby like Eva's, who couldn't wear a two-piece even if she dared. Put some olive oil on the marks and stick a few leaves on them – there – and it'll be fine. Did you see Giorgio before you came up? Did he say anything? He didn't send you up here with the intention of getting me down, did he?'

Three, even two weeks ago, a remark like that from Silvia would have been unthinkable. Irene realized with another little stab of shame that they had begun, very slightly, to drift away from one another. She wondered if Silvia had noticed this too. In a way she hoped she had, in a way she hoped she hadn't. Overcoming a desire to crawl to the edge of the platform, to where the tiles began to slope, and peer over to see if indeed the visibility from the roof was zero, she lay down beside Silvia, peeled her clothes off, and began to talk; listening to herself, and to Silvia's responses, as she would to a gramophone record that had been dropped – to see if it had sustained any damage.

After a while, and particularly when the needle slipped back comfortably into the anti-Giorgio groove, with Silvia listing the most recent defects – 'He funked his last exam.' 'He's spent the money for the children's shoes on a camera.' 'He's rigged up a hammock now, so that he can lie down even when he's in the garden' – and herself adding the 'I know's and 'I heard's and 'I saw's, she decided thankfully that it hadn't. Through no merit of her own, maybe, but the old harmony between them was still intact.

For the rest of the day these flashes of contrition kept occurring (but contrition for *what*, for goodness sake? She had done nothing yet, only look, and what harm was there in that?). When the time came for Giotto's bedtime story, she read it to him sitting on a chair, as far from the window as she could place it. She didn't even approach the shutters until she had finished her reading and turned out the light, and when she did she only allowed herself one quick little glance. Promising herself that it would be the last. Or if not the last, then one of the last.

The terrace too was in darkness and appeared to be deserted, the bathing suits and towels collected, the deck chairs folded away out of sight. So much the better, she told herself sternly, suppressing disappointment before it had time to surface, so much the better.

It was her first conscious step in self-mastery. The others, for reasons which she was careful to conceal from herself until she had found for them an appropriate camouflage, came more easily. After dinner, instead of prowling restlessly round the garden as had become her habit, she sat placidly in the hall with the aunts and cousins, joining in the conversation and listening to the screams of the elder children outside as they played their nightly game of *Tana* (an intricate version of Hide-and-Seek, crossed with Tag and Grandmother's Footsteps and Sardines and indeed almost every other running game Irene had ever heard of). Not once did she fidget, not once did she crane her head round the doorway in the hope of catching a last soothing glimpse of the figure on the terrace, not once, with the excuse of her pregnancy and the heat, did she leap up and disappear into the night to mingle with the players. When she went into her bedroom she bent over Giotto's bed, adjusted the mosquito net and checked that there were no insects on the inside (recently, again to her shame, she had sometimes forgotten to do this and in the morning Giotto had been punctured all over like a pincushion), then undressed and got straight into bed and turned off the light. No wandering around in the darkness, no lingering at the window. No foolishness, in short, because, as she had promised herself earlier, she had put a stop to it.

Her last thought before falling asleep was how easy and how comparatively painless this ending of the ogling had been. Instead of feeling thwarted or deprived, she felt happy. So perhaps there was truth in the platitude, so often uttered by her grandmother, about righteousness bringing its own reward. Of course, there was one small snag involved: having allowed herself to go so far, to compromise herself (and indirectly the family) to such an extent, she must now brace herself to undergo a clarifying meeting with Giuliano in order to explain things to him and ask his forgiveness. It would no doubt be humiliating, certainly for her, possibly for him as well, and quite what to say in the circumstances she didn't know, never having been in them before, but it was something that must be done. It was, to borrow another phrase from her grandmother, a task not to be shirked.

CHAPTER VII

As if already sensing its rarity Irene dealt sparingly with her happiness, determined to make it last as long as possible. With the same instinctive wisdom she also refrained from looking at it too closely. Which meant, patently flimsy as its texture was, that she could hardly look at it at all, merely gather it about her below neck-level like a cloak and wear it while the fabric held out.

For a start there was the fascinating prospect of getting a message through to Giuliano. This, and the composition of the message itself, kept her going for days. She didn't want to make any mistakes in her Italian, either in grammar or spelling, because she felt a linguistic slip-up would sit ill with the high romantic tone she had so far achieved. Each phrase had therefore to be checked several times with several different people before it could go down on paper. 'Eva, which form of address is right for someone of your own age who you don't know? *Tu*, or *lei*, or *voi*?' 'Renzino, how many "p"s in *appuntamento*?' 'Nonna Savia, how do you end a personal letter in Italian? *Distinti saluti*? Are you sure? Isn't that for business letters?' 'Silvia, does *voi* sound stiff to you? Does it sound Fascist? Does it sound common?' And so on, at discreet intervals, until opinions converged and a first tentative draft could be made. Then – in a sense a parallel problem because this information too had to be spelt and written down correctly before the message could be delivered (yet another poser, the delivery. Should she use the post? Pop the envelope in the letter box of the next-door villa herself? Shove it through the bougainvillaea straight into Giuliano's hands? Make a dart with it and launch it on to the terrace?) – there was the equally fascinating question of choosing a suitable meeting place. Not too far: she had seen no car in the Lessings' drive and wasn't even sure she had seen bicycles either, but far enough for safety. Meaning secrecy. Not *too* isolated, or her intentions might be misconstrued, not too crowded either or she and Giuliano wouldn't be able to talk, or whatever it was they wanted to do. It was all delightfully difficult to work out.

With the solution to these and other connected problems – what to wear, what to say, when to act, on what excuse to leave the villa – Irene managed to keep her happiness intact for nearly a fortnight and a half. It was quite a hedonistic feat. Her conscience didn't interfere to spoil things because even on the strictest reckoning there was nothing for it to interfere *with*. Was she not acting rightly? Plotting, yes, but plotting rightly? Making a secret assignment, but making it from the best of motives? In her new-found virtue she had completely given up her observation of the terrace: now that she had decided the course she must follow, such a pastime seemed unworthy of her. This decision dampened her happiness a little, she missed the thrill of the staring bouts and the whizzing and the flickering of the darts, but in compensation it made her feel proud – proud of her strength of mind, of her control, her restored dignity. (And dignity, for one with a paunch the size of the Pope's, had its importance.) She had several times met Giuliano during this period of enforced abstinence, on the path to the beach, on her way to do the shopping, coming out of mass on Sunday morning, but she had barely given him a glance, just smiled quickly and looked away. More virtuous still, she had given up watching the terrace from behind the shutters of her bedroom window, even with the lights off, so she didn't know how he was taking this new attitude of hers; whether he was offended and keeping his own eyes averted in retaliation, or whether he was still hopeful and angling for a glimpse. Not that it mattered much either way, when very soon he would have her letter in his hands, and almost as soon they would be standing alone together face to face, talking to one another, or (she hardly dared make use of the expression again but use it she must, there was no other sufficiently woolly) whatever it was they ended up doing.

With Silvia things had got back on their old comfortable footing, if indeed they had ever been off it, which Irene had now come to doubt. Guilt had no place among her feelings any more, neither actual or remembered. In fact at this particular stage of the proceedings, with the rodent-like craving in abeyance and time running at its normal pace, everything was more comfortable: her everyday life, her dealings with the other members of the family, even the weekend sessions in the bedroom with Tommaso, who, undeterred by her condition, seemed actually spurred by it to become more and more innovative, more and more acrobatic.

Pregnancy, of course, for Italian couples, was traditionally a time for high-jinks on the mattress, Irene knew this well: as Assunta had once put it, reminiscing in a cavalier mood on her own seven gestations, the bill was paid and extras were free of charge so you might as well tuck in as you would in a restaurant. But all the same Irene had to admit that in Tommaso's case there was something very touching in the way he hunched and contorted himself to protect her while busying himself about her pleasure. (Often, nowadays, it must also be admitted, at the total expense of his own.) She had not thought of it in this light before, the sexual act seeming too elementary to need interpretation, but she began to suspect that for Tommaso copulation was not so much the fulfilment of an appetite as an outlet for his generosity. For some reason, probably because it complicated her picture of him when she most needed it to remain simple, she found this idea rather unnerving and did not dwell on it.

Happy though she managed to keep during all this time, fiddling in Penelope fashion over her message, scrapping and re-drafting and relishing the moment (never quite ripe) when she would deliver it, something must have warned Irene that the interval for composition had lasted long enough. Part of her was tempted to ignore the warning and to go on fiddling, but another blunter and more realistic part lost patience and acted; almost, so it seemed to her, subversively, without asking her permission. On the seventeenth day of preparation, with the famous note still only three-quarters finished and the intended meeting-place a set of vague coordinates in her mind – somewhere in Pietrasanta? Somewhere in Viareggio? A café? A cinema? A museum if there was one? – she came back from the beach in mid-morning to find herself totally alone in the garden, and, swiftly, impulsively, scarcely bothering to check if indeed everyone was indoors as it seemed, she crossed over to the wall which separated the two villas and called out, quite calmly if a trifle imperiously, Giuliano's name. Afterwards she could hardly believe what she had done, nor that it should have been so simple.

Two young boys were on the other side, playing ping-pong in the shade of the overhead terrace. Lesser Lessings. They squinted back at Irene uncuriously through the leaves. 'You want Giuliano, Signora?' one of them said. '*Aspetti*. Wait a moment. He's inside, I'll go and call him.' (Signora? Well, of course, that was what she was, and a very large and self-evident one too.)

Seconds later, before Irene had time to think, let along reconsider or retrace her steps, the boy was back again, leading his elder brother by the hand. '*Eccolo*,' he said politely, eschewing the 'Signora' this time, and went back to his game.

And that, after all the heartaches and the hesitations and the days of careful planning, was all there was to it. A straightforward request, a straightforward appearance. Irene was reminded of the theft of a famous picture she had read about recently, in which the thieves, instead of using stealth or violence, had simply turned up at the museum where the painting was housed, dressed in purposeful-looking overalls, and said, 'We have come to take the Titian' (or Tintoretto or whatever it was) 'away,' and taken it. She found herself smiling widely like a clown, invaded by the same irrepressible high spirits as on the day of their first meeting. She was pleased, so pleased she could have shouted, or turned a somersault had her shape allowed it.

Giuliano seemed to be suffering from the same affliction. He bent back a branch of the bougainvillaea, and bringing his face close to the wire-netting that ran along the top of the wall at shoulder-level, smiled back at her with equal foolishness, equal lack of control of the facial muscles. His eyes – a deep violet-blue, she had not reckoned on him having colour on his side as well – shone with amusement, happiness, pleasure, or whatever it was he on his side of the wall was feeling. Irene, who up to then would have sworn she knew the exact cast of his features and could conjure them up in precisest detail with none of the jigsaw problems she had had over Tommaso's, found herself studying them – and not only the eyes – in some surprise. The darkened tooth: she was familiar with that, but it was not on the right where she remembered it but the left. The skin was fairer than she had calculated, much fairer, which made the tooth look even darker. Did it spoil the perfection of the rest? For a moment she thought it did, and then she looked into the incredible eyes again and decided that it didn't, that nothing could, in fact that it actually heightened it. Without the flaw the face, with its clean lines and square jaw and high Aztec cheekbones, would have been too pat, too regular, too conventionally handsome; with it, it took on pathos, personality. It became *his* face and no one else's.

She noticed too that under the face his shoulders were shaking, quite violently, and was uncertain if it was from mirth or emotion until, grasping the wire-netting in his hands and drawing his face closer still, he began to chuckle outright. '*Ebbene*?' he said through the chuckles. '*Ebbene*?'

One of those ductile Italian words, meaning in this case, Irene judged, 'Well, here I am, what do you want from me?' Tinged, perhaps, to avoid seeming too biddable (for she could already see that thralldom did not come easy to him), with just a trace of the more formal, 'Please state your case, please come to the point.'

In spite of the thrill that she felt at his nearness and the desire to prolong it as long as possible, Irene needed no prompting: it was a miracle that the garden was empty at this hour of the morning, and she knew it would not stay that way for long. 'I must see you,' she said, 'that is all. I mean, I think we ought to see each other.'

'Do you?' he replied, still smiling, but countering Irene's impulsive '*tu*' by the third-person form of address, '*lei*', as if to ward her off a little. 'I had the impression recently you thought we ought *not* to see each other.'

So her withdrawal had hurt him. For the first time since the start of their relationship (if such you could call it when this was the nearest to one another they had yet been: three feet apart, across a barrier of chicken wire), it was brought home to Irene that she was dealing with a real human being, not just a beautiful two-dimensional figure in the middle-distance. She found the thought sobering and intoxicating at the same time. 'You know what I mean,' she said. 'I think we ought to meet each other somewhere.'

'So do I,' he said, his hands closing, in what seemed to Irene must be a most painful manner, round the wire.

They looked at one another in silence, trapped in immobility again as on their first encounter, until they were interrupted by a shout from one of the ping-pong players.

'I can't stay long,' Giuliano said, making a slight movement with his head in the direction of his brothers. 'I must go before . . .'

Irene nodded quickly, she didn't want any allusion to furtiveness to sully their dealings with one another at this stage. 'Where shall it be then?' she asked, leaving the choice of meeting-place with him, exactly as she had decided not to.

From the speed with which he answered, it struck her later that he must have given prior thought to the matter. 'Torre del Lago,' he said. 'Puccini's house. It is open to the public now. You will enjoy seeing it. When can you be there? Today? Tomorrow?'

Irene hesitated, flattered but also flustered by his haste. He evidently did not share her opinion about drawing out the pleasures, and this seemed odd to her: she had somehow expected they would have everything in common. 'No,' she said, the word coming out so loud that it sounded almost rude.

'Not today and not tomorrow either. I don't know . . . Later on in the week perhaps.'

He nodded, looking crestfallen and cross, like a child that knows it's being lied to. 'When? Which day?' he urged.

Irene hesitated again, unwilling to commit herself. 'The day you see a red bathing suit hanging out of my window,' she said, delighted by the choreography of this simple and efficient solution until she realized that she didn't possess a red bathing suit. 'No, sorry, I mean the day you see a *green* bathing suit hanging out of my window. On that afternoon I will be there, at Torre del Lago.'

He laughed politely, he clearly did not believe she was serious. 'Like a traffic light?' he said. 'Green for Go?' The simile was probably original because traffic lights in Italy were something very new, but to Irene it sounded hackneyed.

'Exactly,' she replied, feeling suddenly very cheap and foolish, and very irritated with him for making her feel so. 'Green for Go.'

He nodded again before turning away, and the expression in his eyes – vulnerable, beseeching, yet already hardening against her in defence – contrasted violently with the offhand tone of his voice. Irene realized that looks were still far and away their best means of communication: the few words that they had exchanged seemed to have caused nothing but friction and misunderstanding. '*Bon*,' he said lightly, using the French expression, perhaps on account of her foreignness, or perhaps because like most young people he found it dashing. '*Bon*, I'll wait for the green bathing suit. *Aspetto il costume verde*.'

CHAPTER VIII

This meeting, or pre-meeting, or quasi-meeting, with Giuliano took place on a Saturday morning. Irene, who paid little attention to the days of the week when she was in Forte dei Marmi, had no trouble remembering this afterwards because that afternoon Tommaso and his father arrived in the *carrozza* from the station, and they always left the laboratory on Saturday afternoons now that they had no car, there being no fast train in the evening, only a Rapido which in spite of its name wasn't rapid at all. Another reason the day struck in her memory was that that night at dinner Tommaso and Giorgio had the most thunderous row, which, although it seemed insignificant enough at the time, was later to acquire in her mind the divisory structure of a watershed. Upslope and downslope, before and after, and the quarrel like a ridge neatly separated the two periods of her life. Or, more precisely, of Tommaso's life, and thus of her marriage.

They were sitting at table – all eight of them: Renzo at the head, in the patriarchal position he generally tried to avoid, Nonna Savia at the opposite end, Giorgio, Tommaso and Renzino on one side, in this unfortunate order, herself and Silvia on the other, and in between them Renzetto, who had recently been promoted to grown-up supper on a trial basis. Only Olivia and Giotto were absent, already fed and asleep – stowed away in Nonna Savia's huge double bed as on every Saturday in a manoeuvre they were still ingenuous enough to regard as a treat intended for them.

How they got on to the subject of politics Irene wasn't sure. German politics too, which since the war, with its uncomfortable straining of loyalties and its internment camps and its talk of 'Crucchi' and 'Crauti', had become taboo amongst the elder members of the family – something that didn't exist for them any more. Nonna Savia and Renzo, in fact, sat through the entire drama with sad, closed faces, not even protesting when the water jug was overturned in the heat of the argument, only mopping up and tutting their disapproval to themselves.

But anyway, taboo or not, that was unfortunately what happened. Someone, probably Renzino who like all his contemporaries came in for a good bit of indoctrination at school, brought up the topic of the National Socialist assault squads. Irene didn't know much about these, but she knew they had been in the news recently, first because Hindenburg or whoever it was had decided to disband them and then because he had decided *not* to disband them. Or perhaps it was the other way round. Tommaso and Giorgio didn't seem to be all that well acquainted with them either, but this did not matter very much to the ends of the discussion because it soon turned out that it was not National Socialism they were fighting over, but Fascism. Another topic which, apart from the Ciano-Mussolini wedding and the doings of Mussolini's unpopular mistress, the flighty Miss Petacci, was never raised in the family, or if it was, was regularly dropped again on the grounds of its unsuitability for civilized conversation. Giorgio didn't count of course, he would hold forth on anything and the more unsuitable and uncivilized the better, but Irene was quite surprised that Tommaso, raised in this climate of gentle indifference, should hold such evidently strong opinions on the matter.

Excluded from the argument by her ignorance, and suddenly, despite herself, ashamed and cross at being so, she did her best to follow what the two brothers-in-law were saying. Or shouting by now, because both of them had flared up in no time. To some extent her appreciation of essentials, like who was in the right and who was getting the upper hand, was made easier by her not understanding much of their actual words. She doubted terms like '*corporativismo*', '*sindacalismo*', '*pluralismo*' and so forth had much meaning anyway, even to the two users, who appeared simply to spit them at one another like cherry stones: to score and cause offence.

She watched Giorgio, normally so apathetic, so languid in his movements, leap to his feet and begin hammering, auctioneer-like, on the table, his brow furrowed and lumpy, his pale, rather droopy eyes almost circular with rage. He had found another 'ism' now to hurl at Tommaso, that of '*qualuncquismo*', whatever it might be. '*Qualuncquista*!' he shouted when he got to the acme of his invective. '*Qualuncquista*! *Qualuncquista di merda*!' By which – aside from the '*merda*' which needed little translating – he appeared to mean lazy thinking or passive acquiescence in the present system of government. An accusation which Irene couldn't help thinking was rather funny, coming from someone as indolent as him. He believed what he was saying, though, she could see that, believed it ferociously; there was no pose about him now, no superciliousness, no, I am the lone, misunderstood intellectual who has got shut in the chicken run by mistake. He minded, yes, he really minded about Tommaso's dissent. His hands, pulling unchecked at the fringes of the tablecloth, were shaking, his voice had lost its drawl and all its elegant little inflections, the evening was not hot and yet there was sweat on his chin and upper lip; in an incoherent, disorganized, and probably at the end of it, Irene thought, totally fruitless way he was trying to convince his brother-in-law of something that mattered deeply to him. And he was *not* going to be easily done down.

From Giorgio, for once so clear to read, so transparent in his intent, Irene turned to watch Tommaso. He too was extremely angry, but his anger for some reason appeared to be less forceful, less linear in its thrust: despite pulsing veins and flaring nostrils, the bulldozer seemed to have lost its drive. Irene was prepared for his easy victory, which, if politics had anything to do with morals, she knew he deserved because he was good and kind, and a far, far better person altogether than Giorgio was. But victory was strangely slow in coming. For one thing, while Giorgio looked straight into Tommaso's face when he hurled his insults, Tommaso seemed unable to do the same in return, delivering his own to a point somewhere between Giorgio's neck and sternum. A technique which on mere grounds of marksmanship robbed his words of much of their power. And for another thing, Tommaso, unlike Giorgio, seemed not to have his argumentative weapons ready at hand but to be forging them out of chance materials as he went on. And with less and less success, less and less conviction.

As with a dog fight, the sudden shower of water when the jug toppled over signalled a halt to the worst, or at least the noisiest, of the hostilities. After a few more what sounded to Irene rather smug pronouncements about democratic institutions and freedom of expression and what-have-you, delivered more quietly this time, Giorgio sat down, and, with tardy blotches of embarrassment rising on his neck, began mopping up with his table napkin the water that had fallen into his son's plate. Presumably to placate Silvia, who was looking daggers at him because Renzetto, always a tricky eater, had now found the perfect excuse for leaving his food untouched.

Tommaso was silent, he had put his hands to his temples and seemed quite literally to be searching for arguments with his fingers. Apparently in vain.

Nobody said anything for a minute or two: the word *merda* had never made its appearance at table before; Tommaso, to Irene's knowledge, had never been talked down by anyone. Eventually Nonna Savia got to her feet and, with one of those illogical gestures which often mark a crisis, closed the window, murmuring that she hoped the sounds of the row had not reached her brother- and sister-in-laws in the other villas. 'They will think someone has hurt themself,' she explained, no reproach in her voice, just bewilderment. 'We have lived together all these years, Italians and Germans, Catholics and Lutherans, and I never remember a cross word being exchanged between us. Never. They will think an accident has happened and they will worry.' She sat down again, her head shaking gently. It was the closest Irene ever saw her come to speaking ill of the younger generation of the family, which otherwise, at all times and in all its members, she considered perfect.

This speech, perhaps the shame it caused him, seemed to

clear Tommaso's head for him. He took his grandmother's hand, planted a kiss on it by way of apology, mumbled something about never having realized he had a communist for a brother-in-law, and on this Parthian note – *comunista* was as everybody knew a far more shocking word than *merda* – left the table. Irene could tell that despite this forceful exit-line he had suffered a defeat and was making a retreat.

She was only partly right about this, however: it was a defeat, but Tommaso was not running away from it, he was merely distancing himself from it in order to take stock. That evening, for the first time since they had made their appearance by his bedside, she found him engrossed in one of his political books, and in no mood to lay it aside, not even to answer her questions. When she asked, hardly liking to pronounce the word, if Giorgio was really a communist or whether he shouldn't more charitably be described as a socialist, he flipped a hand to silence her. 'Socialist, communist,' he said crossly, 'it makes little difference. He's red and that's all that counts.'

'Whereas you are black, like a piece of an opposing chess team?'

Her flippancy, used to disguise her ignorance, made him even crosser. 'I don't know what colour I am,' he said, turning away from her towards the light and holding the book closer. 'I don't know what colour I am or what shape I am or *what* I am. I only know that there are certain things I believe in, and I want to get them straight in my mind so that I can defend them in the future – to that idiot brother-in-law of mine, or anyone else who cares to challenge them.'

This was said so aggressively that Irene couldn't help asking whether amongst the 'anyones' he also meant her. Not that she had ever expressed any opinions against Fascism – how could she when she didn't have any? – but she knew from her brush with Aunt Frances's *salotto* that English people generally considered Mussolini something of a joke. So perhaps Tommaso thought that she did too, just by virtue of her nationality.

His answer shocked her by its categorical dismissal, rendered even more incisive by the sudden switch to tenderness in his voice. Of course he didn't mean her, he said, laying down the book to stroke her hand. What *was* she thinking of? Of course he didn't mean her. She could no more challenge his political opinions than . . . He paused, looking hard for something equally absurd to balance the comparison. Than . . . than . . . than Silvia could get a degree in mathematics. So there, not to worry. Their countries might disagree, but they themselves would never fall out over politics.

With that he went back to his reading. Irene said nothing, for a moment felt nothing, except for a curious, unlocalized smarting sensation, as if someone had slammed a door in her face or she had done a belly flop. Why not? she asked herself when she had got her thoughts in order again. Why couldn't she argue with Tommaso about politics? Why couldn't Silvia, for that matter, get a degree in mathematics? What was so ridiculous about either hypothesis? Tommaso, no great shakes in debate himself to judge by this evening's performance, had embarked on a course of self-instruction, had he? Well, what prevented her from doing the same?

With an uncomfortable mixture of pride and shame, and hoping that neither showed, she got out of bed and walked round to Tommaso's side where she took a volume at random and took it back with her to read. It turned out to be Gentile – *Philosophy of Art*, or something like that, heavy and sticky as a Christmas pudding. The pages were still uncut, most of them, and she had to get up again and hunt for a pair of scissors to slit them with. (Not, she soon discovered to her increased humiliation, that she needed to slit very many.) Tommaso, deep in his own book, barely noticed.

It was almost the first time since their marriage that they had spent an evening together in this staid, middle-aged way – back to back, each one huddled close to his or her respective light bulb with a nose to print. It was also the first time since her arrival that Irene went to sleep thinking about something other than her unfinished business with Giuliano. (Because she was so frustrated by her failure to understand Gentile's text, and by his habit of using familiar words in an unfamiliar way, that she found herself puzzling over these problems long after she had switched out the light, to the exclusion of all else.) Neither fact, however, struck her as heralding anything of particular significance. The more so because by next morning she had entirely forgotten Gentile and entirely remembered Giuliano, and would continue to do so for quite some time.

CHAPTER IX

She remembered Giuliano with such urgency and single-mindedness because she forgot the bathing suit. Forgot that she had been wearing it on the beach on the Saturday afternoon, and forgot that she had hung it – as she always did with her and Giotto's wet bathing suits – out of the window to dry, last thing at night before she went to bed. Forgot? Well, there again probably part of her forgot and part of her didn't – the human psyche has ingenious ways of getting round itself, better than a boa.

Anyway, forgotten or overlooked or strategically ignored, there it was, on the Sunday morning when she went to open the shutters, a dull olive-green garment (gratuitously large and ugly, like all maternity clothes of the period) drooping innocently from the hook, announcing vivid intentions that she did not have, or was not yet prepared to have. Especially not on a Sunday, with the family *al completo*, and Carmela off with her boyfriend for the afternoon, and privacy about as easy to come by as Aunt Frances's much-envied Earl Grey tea.

She whipped the treacherous suit smartly inside again, hoping she was in time to annul the message: it was only half past eight after all, with any luck Giuliano might still be asleep. The Lessing breakfast was laid out on the terrace as usual, but the only people to be seen were the Admiral and his wife, who sat facing one another at either end of an unusually pristine cloth. It looked indeed as if they might be the first up.

Despite her resolution not to Irene could not help lingering at the window a little to examine them. They looked very plain and elderly, both of them, with white hair and glasses, and a stately, stable way of sitting, as if they had been potted into their chairs like plants. (Giorgio in fact called them the *mezzi busti* and said they had plaster casts of themselves made to put on the terrace for appearance's sake, while their real lives were lived out in riotous dissipation inside the house.) She had difficulty in connecting them to their glamorous, lapis lazuli-eyed son. What would they say, she wondered, if they knew what he was up to behind their dignified backs? They had eight, nine, or was it ten children, they ought to be fairly understanding about such things. But somehow the more she looked at them the more she knew they wouldn't be. On the contrary, they would be shocked out of their skins, horrified, uprooted from their pots. The thought didn't trouble her though in the same way as that of deceiving her own family had troubled her. She didn't know why, but it just didn't. In fact it rather amused her.

She was on the point of leaving the window to wake Tommaso when she saw Giuliano, bounding up the outside staircase that led from the garden to the terrace, to join his parents at their meal. One look was enough to tell her that the damage – if damage it was – had already been done. No one tackled stairs in that fashion, scattering good humour about them like pollen, unless they had scored a victory in love or battle or on the football pools. And if any further proof was needed, when he reached the terrace he lifted his head and looked straight up at her, pointing to where the bathing suit had been and nodding and smiling and making whirling gestures with his hands, as if he didn't care who saw him now or what they thought: the green light had been flashed, and that was all that mattered.

She turned away almost immediately, confused by her ability to affect another person's life like this, at a distance, by means of a botched signal: he looked so happy, so confident, so full of misplaced triumph. And all on her account, on account of spending – what would it be? An hour? Two at the outside – in her company, in a museum or mausoleum or whatever the place was he had chosen. The last hours in her company, what was more; the only hours (although this, of course, he was not yet in a position to know). She realized now that she couldn't possibly disappoint him, that come what may she had somehow to be there. Not Tuesday, not even Monday, but today that ever was. To put him off, even by a day or two, was unthinkable. Besides, she *wanted* to be there. Urgently now, at whatever risk, whatever cost. Even if it meant lying her head off, or taking Giotto with her to the appointment, or confessing everything to Silvia and asking for her help.

In the event it proved unnecessary to do any of these things. As if in tactful connivance with her, the entire household seemed, when the moment came, to adjust itself to Irene's rather questionable requirements. After lunch Tommaso and Giorgio, apparently on the best of terms again after their quarrel, went off fishing, taking Renzo and Renzino with them; announcing as they went (for the benefit of Nonna Savia who worried miserably when any of the family were seaborne) that they did not expect to be back until well after sunset. Nonna Savia, half-way down the corridor on the way to her afternoon rest, called out that in that case she would go and play rummy with Pussi and Tita later on, also until well after sunset: like that no one would have to worry about her worrying.

That was five people taken care of in the space of a minute. Shortly afterwards Silvia, to whom Irene had just decided (and indeed in a rather roundabout way, had already begun) to confess everything, said sorry to interrupt but if Irene didn't mind she thought she would take the children to spend the afternoon with Giorgio's parents: she didn't know why, but she always preferred visiting them *without* Giorgio, the children behaved better for some reason. Could Irene lend her the car? – no, sorry, she was forgetting, Irene had better not be without the car – could Irene drive her over then, and then either stay on and give moral support, or else come and pick her up later, when it was the children's bedtime? Giotto could even remain with his cousins if she liked – he would be no trouble, the house was full of servants, even on a Sunday, because Giorgio's mother was such a dragon of an employer – and Irene could have a free afternoon resting and doing nothing. Perhaps that was the best plan.

No perhaps about it. The plan was so perfect, so unexpectedly, undeservedly perfect, that Irene couldn't help thinking, as she rushed to the bedroom to wake Giotto from his nap and carry out her other preparations (clean teeth, best scent, lipstick, money, dark stripy dress that made her look thinner: lucky she had planned all these things beforehand), that there must be some kind of divine intervention behind it. The flame of her Catholic faith had burnt rather low since she had left England – it was hard to remain a fervent believer in a country where the Pope was called by his surname and spoken of as if he were some kind of overblown MP not overly famed for honesty. But now, just for a moment, it flared up again. Because she was doing right, she felt, God was with her. And to show her He was with her, He had smoothed the path to Torre del Lago for her like a fairy godmother – transport and all. How was one to account, otherwise, for the quite uncannily timely way in which everybody had taken themselves off? She must not take advantage of His bounty, of course, must not waltz too wildly, must not stay too long, but provided she kept her side of the bargain she was sure that – for today at any rate – God would keep His.

By the time she reached the place of appointment, however, she had already begun to doubt the entity of the Almighty's support. When she dropped off Silvia and the children, Giorgio's mother was implacable: Irene must come in, must say hello to the grandmother, must see the house, must have a glass of lemonade. It took her what seemed an eternity to free herself of this unwanted hospitality and drive on again, and when she did she discovered that she had no idea where Puccini's house at Torre del Lago was. She had assumed, the place having only recently been opened to the public and Puccini being the pride of the entire countryside, there would be signs everywhere, but there appeared to be none. Nor, at this the hottest part of the afternoon, and in this one of the wildest spots of the area, was there anyone around to ask. Only birds and insects, and rushes so high and thick that most of the time you couldn't even see the lake from which the place got its name.

Eventually, sweating and swerving, and driving like a hunted hare in frantic lopsided circles, she came across a small handpainted signpost which told her she was (more or less, because the sign was half-fallen and in fact pointed downwards) on the right track. Five minutes and three wrong turnings later, she drew up in a clearing by the lakeside, marked with another dilapidated handwritten sign: '*Parcheggio*'. The lettering was the same as that on the earlier sign, so she judged this must be the place, although there was no other car to be seen, nor bicycle, nor person, nor even, for that matter, house.

There was a path, though, and an arrow to indicate it. This path she took, feeling hot and awkward and already disappointed by Giuliano's unchivalrous behaviour. True, they hadn't mentioned an hour, but he ought, surely, to be there all the earlier on that account; and if he *was* there he ought to be in the clearing, waiting for her.

The path was in fact surprisingly short – only a few yards in length, through another clump of rushes into another clearing – and the house surprisingly close. Very small too, Irene thought, for such a famous man. The whole place appeared to be totally deserted. Her spirits, caught up on the switch-back again like on the day of her first meeting with Giuliano, plunged downwards; then stopped half-way and soared again as she heard his voice calling her from the other side of the house.

It was the first time she had ever heard him use her name. The first time also that she had ever heard it pronounced in completely Italian fashion – 'Ee-ray-nay' – as opposed to the Anglicized 'Eye-ree-nee' which Aunt Tita had schooled all the family, even Tommaso, even the maids, to adopt. The sound enchanted her. Also the difference of the sound, which made her feel freer somehow, as if she had shed, or was now authorized to shed, a part of her identity.

She ran (almost ran: there were significant parts she could not shed) round the house to where Giuliano's voice came from; imagining nothing, but perhaps with a very *arrière-arrière-pensée* of finding him alone and throwing herself, extra kilos and all, into his arms.

He was not alone, though, and she had to brake and quickly compose herself. He was sitting outside what was presumably the caretaker's lodge – an even smaller and more secretive house, built under the lee of the main one and connected to it by a passage – drinking coffee with the caretaker and the caretaker's family. He had been there some time from the looks of it and appeared to be on the very best of terms with his hosts. He also appeared to be deeply and unfeignedly interested in whatever it was they had been talking about together before Irene arrived, because the moment he saw her, instead of getting up to greet her, he merely beckoned her in silence to come and join them at the table.

Irene, under her deliberately vague umbrella-formula of 'whatever it was they ended up doing', had avoided having expectations of any kind about the meeting between herself and Giuliano. All the same, she knew, after ten minutes or so had expired and they were still sitting there at the table, listening to the caretaker chatter on about the 'Maestro' and his looks and his genius and what a good shot he had been and how the Emperor of Japan had sent him countless tokens of his esteem (wait a minute, while he went and got some of them to show them), that she had not expected this.

She would have felt rather offended really, had it not been for the fact that Giuliano was so obviously thrilled to have her beside him and kept squeezing her hand underneath the table when the caretaker and company weren't looking; and had it not also been for the fact that some of the information was actually quite interesting. Even if you didn't give a fig for Puccini, having formed the opinion – goodness knows how or when – that he was flowery and sentimental and in very bad taste.

The caretaker had been the Maestro's gamekeeper, head gamekeeper or *Capo caccia*, as he put it proudly. It was obvious from the way he spoke that the two men had enjoyed a particularly close relationship. He confessed he knew little of the professional side of his employer's life, which was what

Giuliano seemed most interested in, but of the private side he seemed to know a great deal. And also to be strangely willing to reveal it. Most people who came there, he told them, weren't interested in the music, or even the man who wrote it: all they wanted to know about was the scandal of the drowned maid, and whether he had known her, and what she'd looked like, and where she'd jumped, and whether she'd done it out of guilt or innocence, and whether he was the one who had found her afterwards. Or else they wanted to know about the money, and who was going to get it and who wasn't. It was a relief to come across two young people like themselves who didn't ask these sort of questions. And precisely because they hadn't asked, there were one or two things that he could tell them and that they might be quite interested to know. Take the story of the maid, for example. Now that was a wretched business if ever there was one. He had been under-keeper at the time and . . .

With the excuse of scratching a midge bite (no excuse really, because the midges by the lake were terrible), Irene consulted her watch under the table. Many years later, when she had unformed her second-hand opinions on Puccini and formed others of her own, she was to regret not having listened more carefully to what followed. The caretaker's account was fiercely, probably prejudicedly loyal towards Puccini and his wife, Donna Elvira, but even so there might well have been things that an attentive ear might have been able to pick up.

It was hard, however, to lend attention to the love troubles of a deceased Tuscan housemaid when her own were so infinitely more pressing. The caretaker's story seemed to go on for ever, and still Giuliano made no move. Photographs were produced, then, at Giuliano's special request, letters and musical scores. (Of which thankfully it turned out there were very few left in the house.) It must have been a full half-hour before they left the table and began their guided tour of the house, and in the meantime another couple had arrived and tagged on behind. Irene had truly begun to think that the motive of their visit was bona fide sightseeing and nothing else. She was almost caught by surprise, therefore, when, taking advantage of the caretaker's shift of attention to his new visitors, Giuliano slipped his hands round her shoulders from behind and began kissing with what seemed uncontrollable passion the nape of her neck. Even though the move was a logical one, and in a sense what she had come for, it constituted an abrupt, almost strident, change of gear.

He must have registered her surprise and feared her reaction, because when he spoke his voice had a clenched-teeth, don't-do-anything-foolish note to it. Like a kidnapper's, Irene thought, or a bank robber's. 'Let them go ahead into the next room,' he whispered, holding fast her shoulders. 'Don't say anything, don't worry, just let them go.'

Half-heartedly she tried to free herself, thinking how upsetting it would be for the caretaker after all his kindness to catch them profaning the Maestro's memory: she seemed to remember him saying that the composer was buried in one of these rooms, although which one she wasn't sure. A rare privilege, he had said, for a man to be buried in his own house. Accorded only to Kings. Or was it Popes. 'Are you sure it's all right?' she whispered back. 'Don't you think we should – '

'We shouldn't anything,' Giuliano choked into her neck. The caretaker and his susceptibilities did not seem at present to be greatly on his mind. 'Only this, only this.'

When the visit moved on and they were alone he swivelled her round and began kissing her face, her eyes, her mouth, anything he could latch on to, with a pent-up frenzy that would have alarmed her, had she not instantly begun to share it. Her body, despite its shape, seemed to clap to his like iron to a lodestone; she did not know how she could ever bear to draw herself away. Only this. Giuliano was right, she thought, only this mattered, only this existed: to cling to one another and to try to dismantle – by any means, tongue, hands, thighs, spittle – the few slender barriers that still separated them. Who cared about the other couple? Who cared about being seen by them? Who cared about anything?

This in theory. In practice, of course, decorum mattered as well, to both of them, and there followed in consequence perhaps one of the most schizophrenic, disjointed hours of

Irene's life. Certainly of her love-life. The house was minute, the caretaker very thorough, very conscientious. While almost certainly aware of the reason for their lagging behind, he was also aware of what he judged (correctly in Giuliano's case) to be their very real interest in Puccini the musician. As they emerged from each room, bleary-eyed, dishevelled, their mouths bruised and glistening, their minds in some other universe, there he would be, politely waiting in the next, ready to repeat for their benefit the points of interest. The Förster piano, the stool, the pen used for *Butterfly*; the hunting trophies and the stories behind them; the hat, the boots, the favourite gun. Here was a photograph of the Maestro with his son. Which man looked the younger? Why, neither did, they looked like twins; they *were* like twins, only one couldn't play a note. While the other – ah! The other . . .

'A true genius,' Giuliano confirmed enthusiastically at this point, wiping his mouth on his shirt-sleeve and going on to explain, more to himself than any of the others present, what he called Puccini's revolutionary treatment of the operatic form. It amazed Irene the way he was able to transfer his eagerness from herself to the composer with no apparent slackening of tension in between. She herself emerged from each room, and each embrace, in a kind of drunken stupor, able only to prop herself against the wall while the talk went on and to wait impatiently for the moment they would be alone again and able to reunite; he, on the other hand, appeared to switch effortlessly, almost willingly, from lover to tourist and back again, his keenness at maximum in either role. She wished she knew more about him, wished they could sit quietly somewhere and talk while they still had time. Although even as she wished it she knew this was impossible: there was only one way of achieving quietness between them, and that was precluded them, and probably wouldn't work very well anyway, or not for very long.

The dichotomous visit continued. The tomb. Respectful silence, coughings, shufflings, murmurs of, 'What peace, what beautiful glass windows,' from the other two visitors; and then, only seconds later, the cold of the marble on her back and the heat of Giuliano's body on her front as he pressed against the slabs, his temperature febrile, his mouth open, craving for hers. Followed, when his mouth moved downwards, by the sound of his voice, broken, hoarse, muffled, '*Ti prego*, Irene, *ti prego*.' I pray of you. But what prayers could be granted in a tomb? Certainly not these.

On to the kitchen. Lengthy talk about recipes, followed, the moment the others were out of the door, by more desperate groping, and the equally desperate righting of a copper saucepan that almost came unhooked from the wall in the process.

Upstairs (never normally shown but the caretaker was making an exception): the Maestro's dressing gown, the Maestro's bath, the Maestro's bed. And almost immediately afterwards the feel of the Maestro's counterpane beneath her and Giuliano's hand parting her legs and working its way upwards – so surely, so quickly that she had no choice but admit it. The anguished, '*Ti prego*, Irene,' again; bedside prayers this time, but just as difficult to answer. Finally, out into the garden to see the lake, but not the spot of the suicide.

Here at last, in the open, in sight of the others but not too close to them, the conditions of freedom and constraint were of just the right mixture to enable them to talk. Irene, who had not dared to look at her watch but had nevertheless sort of caught sight of it sideways, felt daunted by the prospect. If she opened her mouth at all, she felt, the words would come out like a waterfall, gushing, never stopping. How old are you? In what position do you sleep? In what *room* do you sleep? Which is your window? Do you believe in God? What did you feel when you first saw me? Have you seen my son? Do you mind my being pregnant (waste of time, of course he didn't)? Do you mind my being married (more waste of time, of course he did)? How long are you staying in Forte this year? Where do you live in Florence? What do you do there? In the end, inanely (but then what did it matter what her mouth said when her eyes were carrying on a conversation apart?), she asked him to tell her more about Puccini.

This to some extent he must have done, and to some extent she must have heard him, because years later she was to sit through her first performance of *Bohème* to find little pieces of knowledge drifting down to her, mixed with the snowflakes on the stage, from some store she never knew she possessed. That afternoon, however (evening now), as she drove back alone to Forte dei Marmi, feeling the same sense of loss and outrage that she imagined Renaissance traitors must have felt when their innards were removed and burnt before their noses, she remembered hardly a word. All she remembered was the sound of his voice, and the burning sensation of her hand as it lay between his, and the time passing and the light dimming, and a kind of churning, sick-feeling in her stomach as the moment for saying what she had come to say drew nearer.

Eventually, after another look at her watch – a perpendicular one this time – she said it. A prim, unmeant rigmarole which seemed to come out of her mouth like a conjuror's handkerchief, by trickery, from some foreign source. How she managed to utter it she didn't know, but probably the realization that the churning feeling was in part due to her child moving inside her, helped give her whatever strength – or weakness – she required.

He heard her out in silence. This time he didn't look sad or angry or disappointed, merely submissive. Not to her, Irene realized, but to the moral code she had paid lip-service to which he evidently shared. Or at any rate respected. Or at any rate did not like to be instrumental in breaking or even bending.

She longed for him to do so, almost begged him explicitly to do so, leaving a kind of row of dots or question mark after each 'I cannot', 'It is not right', 'It is not possible', in the hope that he would take her up on it and persuade her how she could or how it was. But with touching, almost irritating rectitude, he only nodded his bleak assent, 'I know. *Capisço*, I understand. I want nothing that you do not want.' They called each other *tu* now, but that, and the trace of her secretion on his hand where it had penetrated her, were the only tangible signs of intimacy that they seemed to have established. A smear of mucus, and a word they had no use for – not much, Irene couldn't help thinking, by way of a souvenir.

As if reading her thoughts, he put his hand to his face when they said goodbye and inhaled deeply, like an ex-smoker with a forbidden cigar. 'I shall never wash it again,' he said. Then, perhaps aware of slipping into the ridiculous, he corrected himself, 'Not tonight anyway.'

Irene was reminded, despite herself, of her grandmother's old head gardener, who had done likewise (with significant variations) after receiving a handshake from Queen Mary. More to delay the moment of parting than anything else, she began confusedly to tell this story to Giuliano, but he seemed merely indignant at her attempt to lighten the atmosphere, and refused to listen.

This minor incomprehension raised a momentary barrier between them which both of them seemed to realize, if ever they were to make the break, they must take advantage of. Quickly, curtly, Irene offered a lift back to Forte dei Marmi which was just as curtly refused, then, without taking her eyes off the road, she slipped the car into gear and drove away. The ragged, unsatisfactory shape of such a leave-taking didn't seem to her to matter a bit. After all, she told herself, the whole relationship between them was ragged and unsatisfactory, and there was nothing either of them could do to trim it. Amputation, whether performed with a scalpel or a hack-saw, was always amputation.

CHAPTER X

A book that occasionally cropped up in family discourse, usually in connection with the solving of crossword puzzles which was the only moment when culture came in any way to the fore, was Silvio Pellico's *Le Mie Prigioni*, My Prisons.

The title came into Irene's mind, unbidden, the moment she closed the gate of the villa behind her after returning from Torre del Lago and collecting Silvia and the children. These, she thought – meaning everything: the garden, the villa, the family itself, even Silvia, even Giotto, even the child inside her, perhaps especially the child inside her – are from this moment forth to be my prisons. In the plural, like Pellico's, because they are several and different. I have sought them out deliberately, drawn them close around me, in two cases brought them into being, and now what do I find? That instead of affording me warmth and protection the way I intended them to, they have transformed themselves into jails and jailers.

Thwarted, furious, disbelieving, she strode up the drive towards the house, feeling (and looking also, she feared, in her striped dress and with her heavy swaying stomach), like a tigress in a cage. No way out, no way out. Bars of her own making on every side.

She disdained to look up at the terrace: she must bear her captivity with dignity, for her sake and for his. He couldn't be back this early anyway. If God would only take the pain away, bring back her happiness, her calm, her contentment with everyday things, she would never look again.

What had she done, oh, what had she done to deserve such punishment?

This restless, caged-beast mood stayed with her all summer long. Tommaso, free from work for most of August, did not know how to deal with her in this state, and left for Florence much earlier than needed, almost a week before the reopening of the laboratory, leaving her as a present a fan and an electric ventilator. He said her pre-natal nerves were catching and he would get more of a holiday on his own in the flat.

Irene was sorry to see him go, but she knew what he meant: she did not get much pleasure from her company herself, crabby and dissatisfied as she had become. She paced and fretted, drawn to the bedroom window despite herself time and time again, but always watching from behind the shutters, never allowing herself to be seen. It was her only weakness, and at the same time her only source of strength. If she caught sight of Giuliano from her hiding place, and if, better still, she caught sight of him (as she occasionally did if she was lucky) looking up at the window, trying in vain to catch a glimpse of her, then for an hour or so, perhaps two, depending on how intense the look she had intercepted had been, she would know something akin to peace of mind. He was still thinking of her, still hers, and she could momentarily relax. The last week in August she bumped into him by mistake at the cycle-repair shop, where she had taken Renzetto's bicycle to have the chain fixed: he wrapped the chain round his wrists right there in front of the puzzled shopkeeper, to mime bondage or the cruelty of Fate or goodness knows what, and gave her a look of such tragi-comic despair that it placated her for the rest of the week.

She got to know the movements of the Lessing family almost as well as those of her own. The villa, like Aunt Pussi's, was divided, she discovered. The top floor belonged to the Admiral's sister, who had a son roughly Giuliano's age and build. Sometimes this son would trespass on to the lower terrace and she would find herself watching him instead, for minutes at a stretch, with the same tension, the same longing, until he turned round and she discovered her mistake. Then she would feel almost ashamed of herself: his face was broader, coarser, he wore a fringe and his eyes were small and porcine; apart from his height and the set of his shoulders he didn't really look like Giuliano at all. How could she ever have thought he did?

She got to know the younger children and their names. She became familiar with the maids, even to the point of knowing that the old fat one who did the ironing didn't use a sprinkler but poured water into her mouth from a glass and then spat it out jubilantly in a spray over the clothes to be ironed. (Should she tell Giuliano this? Was it sufficient excuse for arranging another meeting? Sadly she shouldn't, she decided, and sadly it was not.) She discovered they had two cats, whom the Admiral loved and the maids didn't, as they were always pushing them off the edge of the terrace with their brooms when the Admiral wasn't looking. She found out that Giuliano, and the next in line, Umberto, went diving for Roman remains unbeknownst to their parents – bringing back pieces of vases and amphorae and stuff, and storing them, together with their goggles, in a corner of the garden in a disused water butt. (Their secretiveness over this bothered her slightly. Could it be that the pastime was dangerous? Or did the two brothers simply consider it too childish to be made public? She hoped the latter.) The kitchen she couldn't see from her window, but she usually knew from the smells that wafted upwards what they were having for lunch and dinner. Especially when, as it nearly always was, it was fish. All this knowledge was useless to her, in fact worse than useless, because instead of bringing her closer to Giuliano's life it only served to show her how cut off from it she was, hidden behind a partition of wood, unable to reveal her presence. Nevertheless it constituted a tenuous kind of link with him, and she could not help but continue her watch. Learning more and more, until she could have sat an examination on Lessingology.

At the beginning of September Signora Lessing herself paid her seasonal visit to the aunts, and Irene had difficulty, almost, in greeting her as a stranger. She knew so much about this woman's life, from what she had had for breakfast that morning down to the number and colour of her knickers, it seemed to her virtually impossible that they had never yet met. For fear of saying something she shouldn't she kept unusually silent throughout the visit, disappointing Aunt Tita who had been looking forward to showing her off to their slightly formidable neighbour – one notch above them on the social scale, and decorated by Mussolini with a special fecundity medal. 'What went wrong, *piccola*?' she asked Irene afterwards. 'Didn't you like the handsome Signora Lessing? I will confess to you – *a quattr'occhi*, just between you and me – that I am not *all* that taken by her myself. The way she parades her children down the aisle to communion in their little black uniforms, the way she looks at me when I light up my cigarette . . . There is something rather too good about her, that is what I think. What do you call that in English, when someone is very good, but just a little bit too good to be really good?'

After a moment's reflection Irene said she thought it was called being smug.

'Then she is smuck,' Aunt Tita concluded. '*Un poco poco* smuck. And just between you and me again, it would do her no harm if someone in her family were to do something naughty for a change. It would teach her to lower her crest.' (Aunt Tita's own sons had both liberally obliged her in this regard before they were married, and there were rumours that despite their wives' vigilance they did so still.) 'But they never will, of course,' she added with a touch of melancholy. 'They are such good boys and girls. *Così bravi*. *Così bravi*.'

They were indeed *così bravi*. That was where the trouble lay. But would Irene have felt the way she did about Giuliano had he been less *bravo*, she wondered? She didn't think she would. Her love for him – she had no hesitation now about what to call it: she still wasn't sure what the feeling was, she knew that this was its name – her love for him was directly dependent on his being exactly what he was and behaving exactly as he did. His failure, that day at Torre del Lago, to force her a little further, to violate at least her scruples, had seemed to come almost as a disappointment at the time, but now she recognized it as the fulfilment of a promise. An affair between them at that stage, however passionate, however heady, would have been just an affair: what they were presently involved in (or what they were *not*, to their chagrin, involved in) was something different. They had renounced one another, pushed each other away almost with harshness, and in so doing they had entangled themselves even more deeply. Like a piece of sticking plaster, Irene thought, that you flick from your finger, only to find it adhering to your thumb and then your wrist and then your elbow. Each time closer in, each time harder to remove.

Signora Lessing's visit marked the highest, or lowest, or anyway most galling point of Irene's captivity. That night she was unable to sleep at all. She read for a while, played patience for a while in the deserted living-room with Nonna Savia's cards, padded down to the kitchen once or twice in search of something to eat, and then sat herself on the window-ledge, wrapped in first a sheet and later on, when it turned chilly, in a blanket, and stared out through the slats in the shutters at the darkened terrace below, waiting for the dawn. The cage had grown tighter, smaller; or perhaps it was she who had grown larger. The bars seemed to be pressing against her now, riveted round her chest like the hoops of a barrel. She wanted to scream out, to throw something against Giuliano's window, wake him, tell him she was there and beg him to join her. In fact, as the night progressed, the urge to do so grew so strong that it seemed that if she did not she would burst, or rather cave in under the pressure of the bars. But she did nothing, just sat and sat and sat; only allowing herself to ease open the shutters a little to make room for a pillow to sit on when the window-ledge grew too hard.

The next morning, as if they too had felt the pressure, her waters broke and the birth started. It was not the end of her imprisonment and Irene knew it, but it was a diversion, a change of scene: she was being sent to the prison infirmary.

In fact, as births go, it was rather fun. Cousin Guido, the only male still on holiday, drove Irene back to Florence with wonderful panache, hooting all the way, while Eva, his wife, leant out of the window with a white handkerchief in her hand to signal the emergency to the few cyclists and oxen-carts that threatened to slow their progress. Assunta, never one to miss a drama, came too, and took turns with the handkerchief, filling in the empty moments by checking on the contraction intervals and (depending on how long these were) advising Guido whether to avoid or aim for the bumps.

Intentionally or not, most of the bumps must have been hit, because by the time the car reached the flat, Irene was already having strong expulsive pains. Tommaso and the midwife were there to meet her and to help her upstairs and into bed, and when the midwife saw how advanced things were she packed Tommaso off very firmly – '*Niente maritini.*' We don't want any little husbands around – and took charge herself. Guido and Eva, their hands still poised respectively over hooter and handkerchief, announced they were setting off to fetch the doctor, but were again told by the midwife very firmly that they could if they liked but there was no real need, because by the time the doctor got there it would all be over.

He arrived, in fact, forty minutes later, not quite when everything was over, but almost. Afterwards, seated on the end of Irene's bed, sipping Spumante (Tommaso had tried for champagne but had been unable to get any because foreign goods were already becoming scarce), he congratulated her on the ease with which she had produced this second fine son. 'Perhaps it was all that sea bathing that did the trick,' he said. 'Kept the muscles trim. A shame that you won't be able to do any more of it, but there you are. Babies come first, don't they, in all mothers' considerations? *I bambini avanti a tutto.*'

Irene smiled, and then stopped smiling, struck by something disturbing in the doctor's words. She asked him to explain what he meant. Why couldn't she swim any more? Was she no longer watertight or something after two confinements?

The doctor laughed, so did the midwife. Both speaking at once they explained to her there was nothing wrong with her, it was simply that she wouldn't be able to swim because in Florence there wasn't any sea to swim in. She had a newborn baby to look after, the doctor went on, evidently aware from Irene's puzzled expression that a more scientific approach was needed, and it was common knowledge (although perhaps not common knowledge in England, or Sparta for that matter) that babies could not be taken to the seaside until they were at least three months old. It was extremely bad for them, there was too much iodine in the air. The midwife nodded. Even Tommaso seemed, in a neutral way, to agree.

Despite the feeling of panic rising in her throat at the thought of being unable to return to Forte dei Marmi and her lookout post at the window, Irene couldn't help laughing. What about the babies that were born by the sea, she asked? What about island-dwellers? What about the women that lived on Capri? Did they all move to the mainland when they were expecting?

The doctor looked rather put out. Necessity was a different matter, he said. And then she must remember that coastal areas had coastal populations, inured to iodine, or else disfigured by goitres. Certainly there was no mortal danger involved, but having the choice of an inland residence and a seaside residence, it was highly preferable that the baby should spend, if not the first months, then at least the first weeks of its life in the former.

Irene remained sceptical, but the possibility, however remote, of her tiny, defenceless son developing a goitre through her own selfishness was even more abhorrent to her than exile from Forte dei Marmi, no matter how prolonged. She wished the doctor had never mentioned goitres. A cold to the baby she would have risked, sunrash too, even freckles, even a squint perhaps, but a goitre, no, that she could not contemplate. It pleased her to discover this, because she was so unsure of her priorities nowadays that she hardly ever dared inspect them, for fear of finding herself to be a closet-Medea.

In a way the ban on movement quietened her, focused her attention for her, like blinkers on a nervous horse. Freed from the servitude of the window-watching, she could concentrate on other things, unconnected with Giuliano, unconnected, to some extent, with herself. She read a lot: there were more and more books in the flat, she noticed, some of them by authors she had never heard of, others by writers she knew to be in exile or on the Index or at any rate out of grace with the regime. She discussed what she had read afterwards with Tommaso, who surprised her by the amount of knowledge he seemed to have acquired since his clash with Giorgio: he had grown into quite an expert now, not only on the National Socialist Party in Germany, but on politics in general. He had developed all sorts of theories on power and wealth and the class system and why the rich were rich and the poor poor, and seemed determined to put them into practice in order to better the lot of the people working for him. Irene found herself listening to him, for the first time since their marriage, with genuine interest. Mixed, too, with a certain, almost furtive, admiration. Not only because she approved of his new ideas – which by and large she did, although some of them, particularly those on class division and the exploitation of labour, seemed oversimple to her, and his acceptance of them too hasty – but because she approved of the new person they seemed to have turned him into. His clothes were scruffier now and looked better on him as a result; his way of treating her was more off-hand but at the same time more companionable; his deafness in her regard, although liable to overtake him in the evenings, when the baby slept and they were stretched out together on the bed, seemed to be largely cured. Not only did she listen to him, that is, but he listened to her as well. They argued a lot, which they had never done before; they discussed religion, which they had never done before, deciding by the end of it that their attitude needed thoroughly overhauling. They even began, in a homespun way, to attempt the overhaul.

In addition to these new-found intellectual pursuits she had the baby to look after, although what with Assunta and her regular Florence helpers, and no Giotto on her hands for the time being, the care of just one small, relatively immobile child was a cinch. And she had baptism to see to. Not to attend, because as the mother she was for some reason or other denied access to the church, but to organize from the point of view of food and entertainment. Particularly of food.

The family returned *en masse* for this occasion, coinciding as it did, more or less, with the re-opening of the schools. They brought with them a whiff of the sea and a sharp recurrence of Irene's unease. There had been an end-of-season party on the beach, Silvia told her in great excitement as soon as they were alone together. Everyone had come, all the neighbours, all the regular beach-goers, decked out in fancy dress, and they had lit fires and cooked shellfish and danced and had a whale of a time. Even Giorgio had admitted under pressure that it had been fun. Renzino had been found smoking with two other boys in the *bagnino's* cabin. Blacky had eaten, and then shat out again intact with no ill effects (Renzetto had counted them) twenty-nine mussel shells. Eva's eldest daughter, Monica, had made a dead set at Giuliano Lessing, who had come dressed as a sheikh – not very original but, goodness, he did look terrific: everyone agreed it was the first sign of good taste Monica had ever shown. Eva had packed her off to bed and then gone all languid and danced the tango with her shoes off, even though her costume was Tyrolean. Signora Longari had bared her midriff and come as Salomé. Uncle Otto had challenged Dr Fersten to a rowing match and both of them had nearly passed out from the effort. Oh, and a dozen other dramas had taken place, particularly on the sentimental plane: all the young giving their elders the slip and sloping off into the pines to misbehave. How she wished Irene had been there, they would have had such laughs.

As she listened, all Irene's restlessness came back with a vengeance. Accompanied by the same feeling of unworthiness she had experienced earlier in the summer. The christening ceremony, in which she was unable to partake, seemed only to highlight her condition of pariah, of outcast on sexual grounds. It was right, she felt, that only the clean be admitted into the church, and that she, in her presently grubby state, be excluded. It was right because she had been given all the ingredients for happiness – to which another one had just been added – and she was unable to make anything of them. All she could do was to sit there like a cussed cook on strike and hold out for the one incompatible ingredient she could never have. The incident with Monica, who was fifteen and covered with puppy fat and not even very pretty underneath it, filled her with what she first took to be jealousy but soon realized was envy: envy of her youth and innocence and of her freedom to approach Giuliano openly and make public her feelings. Whereas Irene's own – far deeper, far more serious – had to be concealed like a blemish or a case of tuberculosis.

Because that was how things stood. Seen from the outside this was a moment of achievement – a second beautiful healthy child born to her in record time, her family round her to celebrate, more presents on the way, and Unclo Otto busy on a second poem, already thumbing through the dictionary for words to rhyme with Francesco, which was the name she and Tommaso had chosen. Seen from a closer, more individual, viewpoint the picture was still attractive: Silvia was back, Giotto was back, Irene had found a subject to apply her mind to outside the confines of the house and family (indeed that winter she thought she might even enrol in university alongside Giorgio to study political sciences or whatever his subject was called: her ignorance of history and economics was still appalling), and life with Tommaso was in consequence changing into something more challenging, less predictable. As was Tommaso himself. Yet from the innermost viewpoint of all there was nothing – just a great gaping wound where the severance from Giuliano had been effected, begging medication, or else reunion with its amputated part.

CHAPTER XI

The christening party was reckoned by everybody a great success. By everybody, that is, save for Irene herself who couldn't help feeling ill at ease in the position of Mater Gloriosa, and possibly Giotto who, swamped by jealousy, spent the whole time crawling around on all fours between the guests' legs pretending he had forgotten how to walk. (Renzetto and Olivia in turn found this behaviour so witty, they couldn't resist copying it, which made for a certain amount of tension among the servers.) Aunt Frances came, conciliatory, well disposed – particularly towards the male members of the family – and under the mistaken impression, which no one seemed to have the heart to put her right about, that the new baby had been named after her.

There were one or two resurgences of her old disapproval: when Aunt Pussi drove her into a corner, for example, and began dispensing trustworthy remedies for constipation, ending up with her favourite, '*Avec le doigt*, Signora Frances, when all else fails, do you understand? *Avec le doigt*, *il dito*, ze finger.' Or when Uncle Otto, high on Spumante, began describing to her in what was intended to be flattering, confidential detail the pros and cons of his proposed prostate operation due to take place next spring. On both these occasions Irene caught her aunt eyeing her in acute distaste mixed with wonder, as much as to say, How can you, Irene, put up with this sort of thing – this earthiness, this lack of finesse? But by and large the sheer sincerity of the family and their utter failure to register these, or indeed any other attempts at criticism on her part, seemed to have won Aunt Frances over. Or perhaps worn her down.

She stayed until the end and wound up on the sofà with Tita's elder son, the enterprising Marco, watching, with no apparent censure this time for his lack of finesse, while he showed her how to remove any eventual wine stains that might have fallen into her lap or on to her bodice.

'I think you are very lucky really,' she said to Irene on leaving. 'Underneath it all they are poppets, most of them. And I hear things are going *rather* well, businesswise I mean. The new liver tonic and whatnot . . . I've seen advertisements all over the place. Yes, I think, all said and done, you're quite a lucky girl. Come and see me next Wednesday if you are still here, and bring that nice Whatever-his-name-is I was getting along so well with.'

It was an olive branch, Irene supposed. Not a very leafy one because Tommaso had not been invited, but nevertheless an olive branch. She had no intention of accepting the invitation, however, first because she had resolved never to attend another of her aunt's Wednesdays in her life, and second because she had also resolved, now that the prescribed period of quarantine had elapsed, to return to Forte dei Marmi in the hopes that Giuliano would still be there; and to remain there, window-gazing to her heart's discontent, until the start of the university term, which began even later than the school one, sometime in mid-November.

Next morning, however, she woke with a fever, to discover she had developed mastitis and was in no state to travel. Although she and Tommaso were fairly well advanced by now in the process of sloughing their religious beliefs, it seemed again to Irene like an intervention on the part of her half-discarded God – this time a punitive one. A slamming of the gates of paradise, or in this case of the windows. There seemed nothing for it but to pick up the threads of her Florence life and see if she couldn't weave them into some tolerable kind of pattern.

With Silvia for company, and the children to look after, and her political education to further, it seemed a not impossible task. To keep busy was the important thing, she discovered. The ache was still there, but if you could find enough things to do during the day and go to bed at night sufficiently tired, it had less chance of making itself felt. On one of their visits to the park the children found a little mongrel puppy, suffering badly from hunger and exposure: Irene had not thought yet of having a dog of her own but she added it gladly to the household, not on the principle the more the merrier but the more the less miserable – with herself, more than the dog, in mind. Finding herself slightly out of step with Tommaso on the question of religion, which he seemed to be able to jettison without a qualm but which she still had difficulty in relinquishing entirely, she also took to going to church fairly regularly and to talking to one of the priests there about her impending apostasy. The priest in question was young and handsome and had a look of Giuliano about him, especially in the eyes, so these visits were not quite as useful as they might have been in keeping her mind off things, but anyway they took up time.

When the university re-opened she went to make enquiries about enrolling and learnt that in order to qualify for the subject she had chosen she must sit for what was called the Maturità Classica. This meant taking coaching in Greek and Latin and mugging up on a five-year syllabus foreign to her in more than one sense. Tommaso looked at her almost pityingly when she told him her intentions: the Maturità held terrors in Italy similar to those aroused by the guillotine in France. But Irene was undeterred and set about finding herself a tutor: more things to do, more things to think about, less time to pine.

Children's walks, dog walks; baby food, puppy food; discussions with Padre Domenico, discussions with Tommaso, reading, studying, cramming with the tutor, dressmaking with Silvia, toffeemaking with Silvia, the making of everything she could think of with Silvia – it worked, for a while. Towards Christmas, however, perhaps because Aunt Frances roped her into an evening of carol-singing that made her maudlin, or perhaps simply because her normal routine was interrupted, the pain returned with such violence, and the urge to see Giuliano became so strong, that Irene found herself late one night leaving her bed almost unwittingly, like a sleepwalker or a zombie, and seizing the telephone directory and leafing through it in search of his address and telephone number. With the intention (presumably, for what other purpose could the knowledge of his whereabouts serve?) of getting in touch with him, or at least bringing herself into geographical proximity to the area in which he lived.

In order to put some kind of external check on herself, she did what she had been wanting to do for a long time and let Silvia in on her secret. The telling came as a great solace, like the lancing of a boil or the cutting of an abscess. It was a relief just to be able to speak Giuliano's name, but to go through, as Silvia insisted she should, the various snail-pace stages of the romance, day by day, look by look, *frisson* by *frisson*, was more than a relief, it was a temporary cure – like reliving them all over again in another, admittedly more cramped, dimension.

From the point of view of moral buttressing, however, it proved a mistake. Silvia was not only understanding, she was thrilled to pieces by the news. But didn't Irene realize, she kept on saying, it was a *conquista*! She had made a conquest! Never mind the boring old shoulds and shouldn'ts, there would be time for those later: the fact was that all the girls had been after Giuliano Lessing for years – look at Monica, for example, the way she'd set her cap at him at the beach party – and yet it was Irene, husband and all, tummy and all, who had caught him.

Silvia's glee was genuine, but it seemed to Irene that it had more to do with the implications of the conquest than the conquest itself. Then there is hope for us yet, was the lesson Silvia appeared to draw from it: we are still young, both of us, we are still pretty, in spite of the prams and the pots and the nappies, that chapter of life is not closed for us. In consequence she was almost as reluctant as Irene was to look on the affair as finished. When pressed – 'Should I go on seeing him behind Tommaso's back then? Is that what you are suggesting? That I take him as my lover and blow the consequences?' – she merely wrinkled up her nose and told Irene not to be so melodramatic, of course she wasn't suggesting anything of the kind, she was merely saying she didn't see the point of breaking things off so completely the way she and Giuliano had done. Surely it was better to keep in touch in a neighbourly sort of way, see one another now and again, visit a few more museums and whatnots, and let things die a natural death?

Irene did not realize this immediately, but in fact Silvia's attitude over this matter caused a slight – a very slight – rift in their friendship, destined to last for several years and only to mend in the most fluky and unpremeditated of ways. There was nothing to reproach her with, save if anything an excess of female loyalty and generosity, but somehow it gradually became clear that, despite their incessant chattering on every subject under the sun, when it came to matrimonial morals they did not share the same language. Or perhaps it would be more exact to say the same logic: Irene's system had two values, true and false, while Silvia's appeared to have many more. Far from discouraging Irene from making contact with Giuliano, in the days that followed it was she, Silvia, who urged that they go a little further in their outings with the children, into the district where the Lessing family lived, and as was bound to happen, after a few unsuccessful attempts they met him.

He was walking towards them on their side of the pavement, wheeling a bicycle with such a large, parcel-filled basket attached to its handlebars that for a moment Irene mistook him for a delivery boy. In his winter version, muffled in a scarf and wearing a worn, old-fashioned overcoat that must have come down to him from an elder relative, he looked quite different: less arresting, less immediately attractive. You had to watch the faces of the other women as they encountered him, and note the starts that they gave and the quick furtive glances of appraisal, to realize that the allure was still there, under all the wool. (He looked too, Irene thought when he drew nearer, as if he might have a filthy cold, and she latched on to this piece of semi-information greedily, as if the knowledge constituted a bond which would last as long as the germ did. She half-wished – but only half – she could come close enough to catch it.)

Realizing that she was not alone he did not stop or give any sign of having recognized her, bar a slight wobble of the bike as he passed, but her presence in his home territory must have given him cause for hope. From that moment on he began, very timidly at first, very discreetly, to lay a kind of long-distance siege. Silent telephone calls started to arrive – usually in the morning, shortly after Tommaso had left for work – perplexing the cleaning lady whose duty, and also pleasure, it was to answer them: the ringing of the telephone was still something of an event in those days. 'Your secret admirer again, Signora Irene,' she would say, hooting with laughter, because her fondness for Irene prevented her from thinking such a thing could be true. Then hand-delivered notes began to come, brought up by the *portiere*, who from the blank expression on his face when he passed them over seemed to think that such a thing not only could be true but was. 'Will call on the dot of four-thirty, please answer the telephone yourself if you can.' 'Imagine the afternoon is not a good time, will call tomorrow morning, nine twenty-two.' 'Are you never alone? You must be sometimes. Tell me when, so that I can ring safely.'

It was the prelude to a spate of appointments, telephonic and otherwise, conducted on the verge of irresponsibility, almost of wilful disclosure. They arranged a code, shameful in its simplicity: Giuliano would prefix his calls with a single ring, Irene would answer them if she was alone with the word *Sì*, with the word *Pronto*, if she wasn't. Since Carmela and the cleaning lady, and the laundry lady for that matter, all used the more formal *Pronto*, when Giuliano heard that response he was to hang up immediately. (And when and if he heard Tommaso's voice he was to hang up sooner than immediately, but that went without saying.) They arranged meeting-places: a corridor in the Uffizi with a recess, half hidden by a pillar, where they could stand glued to one another for minutes on end without anybody taking particular notice; a table in a café frequented by billiard players where the lights were low and the public incurious; a crescent-shaped yew hedge in the Bobboli Gardens – safest of all but cold; an entire floor of the Palazzo Pitti where the late-nineteenth-century landscapes were on show, which nobody ever bothered to visit. In one or other of the places, rotating them so as to be less conspicuous, they met each other on an almost weekly basis throughout the winter and spring, sometimes for an hour or longer, sometimes for only tantalizing minutes. Florence was small, parochial in those days, and the risk of recognition was high, hence the careful choice of rendezvous, but once they were in each other's company it seemed to be impossible, unthinkable, to worry any further about concealment. They had eyes and ears and consideration only for one another.

Afterwards, in the bleak period, when the store of memories had become for her like a set of iron rations – something to hoard jealously and consume only in moments of desperate need – Irene would try to remember what exactly they had talked about in all these stolen hours they spent together, but found the retrieval work strangely difficult and unrewarding. Clearer in her mind were the things they had not talked about and why: not her home life because Giuliano said he couldn't bear knowing what she did when she was not with him; not his home life for the same reason on her side; not the future because there seemed to be no room in it for either of them; and definitely not politics, because on the one occasion she had broached the subject he had just laughed and told her he had no time to worry about improving world affairs when his own were in such a mess. 'You're a religious agnostic, aren't you?' he said. 'Well, I'm a political one. Fascism may be wrong, liberalism may be right, the socialism you get so worked up about may even be righter, but frankly I couldn't care less. Lecture me if you like, because I love the look on your face when you turn so serious and *passionaria*, but don't expect to win me over. You know what a friend of my cousin's told me last summer when we were walking past your villa after you'd left? He said, "That's the home of the young Fortini couple. The husband's so red he'd sell his grandmother to the Russians for the price of a sticking plaster, and the wife's so stupid she does everything he tells her. They've just had a baby and called it after Lenin." And you know what I said in your defence? Nothing at all. And you know why? Not because I was afraid of letting on how well I knew you, but because the whole thing just seemed too futile and irrelevant to waste my breath on.'

No future, very little present: this seemed to leave them with the past as the only possible area of discourse, but Irene couldn't remember them talking much about that either. So, mostly, she supposed, although in retrospect it sounded jejune, and hardly sufficient fuel for one conversation, let alone dozens, they must have talked about themselves and the impasse in which they were stuck. Virtually every meeting was a leave-taking or a renunciation of some kind, never once (although mostly for logistic reasons and not for want of trying) did they reach the physical closeness they had attained on the Maestro Puccini's bed. But the sheer number of their goodbyes and *addios* brought with it a certain sense of security, and they quitted one another each time with less and less drama, and less and less conviction. Their words implied the opposite, but it was nevertheless clear that time was bringing them, and would continue to bring them, closer and closer together.

With what seemed to her afterwards incredible levity, Irene would get out of bed at night when Tommaso was asleep and creep towards the telephone to dial Giuliano's number. The first time she did this, without meaning to she raised the entire Lessing household: the late-night call was interpreted as a sign of disaster, and to her surprise and Giuliano's embarrassment the whole family flocked to the telephone in their nightclothes, wailing and sobbing and trying to wrest the receiver from him in order to know the worst. 'It can't be a girlfriend,' Irene overheard his mother say, in reply to his reassurance that the call was for him and had nothing to do with grandmother falling down or grandfather being taken ill. 'No girl in her right mind would do a cruel, thoughtless thing like that.' And then, after a short pause, more tartly, 'But if it is, then I never want you to bring her here.' No danger of that, Irene felt like telling her, no danger of that.

Tommaso woke up only once to find the bed empty, and accepted without query Irene's explanation that she had been to get a drink of water. He was working hard, and worrying hard about events in Germany and riots in Spain and similar things, and when he slept he slept heavily. He made love to her less often too, which Irene accepted as a welcome simplification.

She had little time and little inclination, really, to look on Tommaso as a separate person: to do so would have meant inspecting her feelings about him, and this she was at present not prepared to do. Even so, she had to admit that he had grown into a very different person now from the bland, even-tempered, faintly wooden young man she had married. His relations with his own family had changed too, it was hard to say whether for better or worse, although the family, with the staunch exception of Nonna Savia, would probably have said for worse. He had become more impatient with them, with their calm, their gentleness, their detachment from the political arena. Recently, at one of the Sunday gatherings, he had snatched up a magazine that was lying on the table and had begun reading out excerpts from it in a loud, caustic voice, quite unlike the one he normally used in their presence: 'A man has walked on stilts from Graz to Budapest, encountering cheering crowds all along his route.' 'The Carnival this year in Viareggio was magnificent as ever, in spite of the restrictions on building materials for the floats. Tins, rags, papier mâché, the odd piece of driftwood and lashings of Italian fantasy, made of this year's procession one of the most sumptuous on record. Particularly admired by the crowds, gathered from all over Italy for the occasion, was the majestic "Wine Harvest", representing one of our country's merriest but most noble traditions.' 'In Australia, where summer comes in winter and, as is well known, everything is back to front and upside down, a group of bathers have invented a "slowness" race, riding on the backs of giant sea-tortoises. Last past the buoy is awarded first prize and loser takes all!'

By the time he got to the third excerpt the irony in Tommaso's voice had reached such a pitch that everyone in the room had stopped talking in order to listen. 'And *this* is the news you read?' he flung at them in disgust. 'This is how you keep abreast of the times? In your beloved Germany a vulgar, scheming gangster comes to power, his thugs burn the Reichstag and blame it on the communists, people are thrown wrongly into prison, civil rights are suspended and the press is gagged; in Italy our own home-grown gangster behaves in much the same fashion; and you sit here reading about carnival floats and giant tortoises? What has come over you all, for goodness sake? What have you done with your brains? Pawned them? Put them away in mothballs?'

His outburst was greeted by a shocked silence. Giorgio's role of gadfly the family had learnt to deal with, it was accepted as part of his *carattere*, just Giorgio being Giorgio, but criticism from Tommaso was another matter. Tommaso had practically taken over from Renzo the running of the laboratory now, Tommaso was dependable, Tommaso was a mainstay of the family; surely, Irene could almost hear them thinking, he wasn't going to turn into a firebrand and put all their hard-won fortunes at risk? Uncle Otto turned pink and for want of better occupation bent to tie his shoelaces which seemed all of a sudden to have come undone. The aunts and female cousins busied themselves about the laying of the table. The children laughed, genuinely amused by the idea of the tortoise race. Only Guido retaliated, by snatching up in turn Tommaso's copy of the *Osservatore Romano*, the Vatican newspaper which according to Tommaso was the only one still to carry a certain amount of reliable foreign news, and pretending to wipe his bottom on it. This was shocking in another way, and on a note of double disapproval, mixed with something that seemed to Irene akin to actual fear, the family sat down to what was to prove the first of many conflictual Sunday lunches.

Irene's loyalty towards Tommaso by her own admission was very faulty, and now that she had her exam syllabus to study she had little time to keep up with current affairs. Nevertheless in these Sunday bickerings she found herself more and more openly taking Tommaso's side. Her popularity in the family did not suffer as a result because it was somehow looked on as inevitable and even fitting that a wife should second her husband's ideas, but her position shifted slightly, and as the weeks passed the four of them – Tommaso and herself, Silvia and Giorgio – began increasingly to form a group of their own within the group: loved, accepted, incorporated, protected from outside attack, but for all that a thing apart. *I nostri giovani ribelli*, as Nonna Savia took to calling them fondly, our young rebels. *I nostri giovani cretini*, as the rest of the family called them less fondly, our young clots.

CHAPTER XII

Late that spring, on the eve of her fifth departure for Forte dei Marmi, which this year she had been trying to put off for as long as possible in order not to have to interrupt altogether her recurrent adieux with Giuliano, Irene had her last conversation with Padre Domenico and gave up religion for good.

Although it was the first unpopular move she had made (or made openly) as far as the family was concerned, and although even the Lutheran contingent clucked and shook their heads and said it was a pity, and a grave social handicap for the children to have a Godless mother, she felt lighthearted about it. Mainly, or so she told herself, because it signified intellectual freedom, growing up, shaking off the rusty old chains her brain had been shackled in for so long. But also because in a surreptitious way she couldn't help hoping it would bring with it freedom of another kind. What was adultery if it was no longer a sin? A pastime. And what was wrong with it if no one knew about it? Nothing, surely, nothing at all.

Padre Domenico seemed to guess something of what was going through her mind, although she had never spoken to him of her personal troubles, only her doubts and theological snarls. On account of the eyes, their relationship had always had a slight undercurrent of sexuality about it. 'Think things over carefully, Irene,' he urged, taking her hand and giving a significant little tap to her wedding ring. 'Life will not be easier for you without faith, it will be more difficult. You will need more courage, and having no God to turn to you will not know where to find it. If you feel yourself giving in to temptation – and a young woman like yourself is bound to come across many temptations – remember that I am always here, willing to listen and to give you all the help I can.'

Kind words, but by now irrelevant: temptation had no meaning outside the context of sin, and sin was what Irene reckoned she had got rid of with all the rest of the unwanted Catholic luggage. In the flurry of departure, she was unable to arrange another meeting with Giuliano to tell him of her change of heart (or change of soul, or mind, or conscience or whatever, because the heart couldn't really be said to have changed at all), but had to be content with delivering her message of surrender over the telephone the morning she was leaving. Perhaps on account of the medium, perhaps on account of the hour and the possibility on either side of being interrupted, the exchange was curiously gruff and businesslike in character. Indeed it occurred to Irene later that there was something almost necessarily arid in promising to become someone's mistress at a later date and not at the moment when the promise was given.

Giuliano let out no whoops, no cries of triumph, merely registered the news diligently, much as one would that of the arrival of a parcel for later collection. 'So it looks as if I'll manage to get through the summer after all,' was all he said by way of jubilation. 'I thought I would have to travel, make some excuse to my family and just get out of the place. But if things are as you say, then I suppose I can hold out a few months more.'

'Things are as I say,' Irene assured him. 'I have never gone back on my word. Things are as I say. For us to meet in Forte is out of the question and you know it. Where would we go? How could we get there without being seen? But find somewhere for us in Florence in the autumn and I will come there. You know that it won't be often, and you know that I won't always be able to stay very long, but I promise that I will come.'

Giuliano gave a brief snort and said something rather dispirited about having few friends with enough money for places of their own, and fewer still that he could trust, but that nevertheless when the time drew nearer he would start looking. Making it sound, Irene thought, as if she had entrusted him with a chore.

They closed on what seemed to her an even more unsatisfactory note. Just as she was preparing to say goodbye, having at last managed to charge her voice with some of the passion she felt was appropriate to the occasion, the puppy came close to the telephone and began chewing the wire. She chased it away crossly with a '*Pussa via, stupido*!' and heard Giuliano give an intake of breath, so pained and disapproving that it surprised her. 'Don't speak to him like that, Irene, I beg of you,' he said. 'I hate to hear you speak to him so harshly.'

Piqued, because she in fact doted on the animal and had never before chided it except for its own good, she snapped back at Giuliano rather childishly not to be so stuffy and that she could say what she liked to whoever she liked, and rang off in a huff. It was only later, during the journey, when she had time to reflect on the incident, that she realized he must have thought she had been speaking to Giotto, not the dog. And it was later still before her initial amusement over the misunderstanding began to wear off and she began to discern in it slightly more serious implications: namely, that Giuliano could not know her all that well if he thought her capable of such behaviour towards her own child, nor regard her very highly, nor link, as she did, his love for her body to his love for her character. These things, however, she found not so much uncomfortable as unnecessary to dwell on, and with a determined reuse of the comic label she put the whole foolish episode out of her mind.

Her fears about the cut-and-dried nature of the arrangement she and Giuliano had reached dissolved as the summer progressed. In fact, quite to the contrary, the secret pact between them overlaid the days and the nights, the weeks and the months, with a deep, rich, comforting bloom of eroticism, under which everything and everyone they came in contact with appeared to flourish, to ripen, to prosper. The exchange of looks was important but no longer urgent; it came, when it came, as a bonus, as cream on an already delicious chocolate soufflé. The misunderstandings, the awkwardness between them might never have been: they were again in a state of aesthetic grace.

They met in the town, in the sea, on the path to the beach, greeting one another with quick tangential smiles to offset their outward show of indifference. Giuliano came to deliver his mother's note announcing her regular yearly visit and was drawn by the aunts into the radius of the knitting circle, where he sat for what they afterwards declared an inordinately polite length of time, charming everybody – except Irene of course, whom he studiedly ignored throughout. They sat in adjacent rows in the open-air cinema, and during the performance Giuliano bent forward to pick up his jersey, brushing his lips against Irene's hair as he did so and murmuring her name. They ran into one another at the ice-cream kiosk by the jetty, each with a child in tow, and lingered there, exchanging grins and mouthing silent messages of love over the children's heads. The wing of their contract extended itself over them like a warm protective covering, quieting impatience, annulling frustration, making separation itself almost a pleasure of the senses.

People, weather, events, even world events, seemed to conform to the same benevolent pattern. Irene and Giuliano were not the only ones to reach an agreement: in the beginning of June Mussolini announced to his muzzled Senate the signing of a four-sided pact between the principal western powers with the aim of promoting peace and providing mutual aid. Even Tommaso seemed to find the news reassuring. The dining-room wireless set was brought out into the garden for the occasion on a long lead of plugs and cables, so that the knitters could follow the Duce's words without downing their needles, and everyone sat round listening and nodding in relief and approval. Italy, Germany, England, the three nations that most closely concerned them, uniting with America to form a quadruple bulwark against war and disorder: it was as things ought to be, everybody behaving well and sensibly, even Hitler who evidently wasn't quite as bad as he was made out to be. The Duce's speech ended on an unaccustomedly religious note: 'The clouds have been gathering on the horizon,' he proclaimed in his vibrant, tangy voice with its Emilian accent the aunts so deplored, 'but now they part to admit a luminous ray. May He who is Lord of all Governments allow to pass through this opening not only the hopes but the certainties of the peoples of this world.' Accent forgiven, the aunts settled back contentedly in their chairs: so Mussolini too was learning to behave in a responsible, decorous fashion; *certain young people*, they would not say who, might do well to take a leaf from his book instead of criticizing the way they did.

Towards the end of the month the *al fresco* wireless set was rigged up again, this time to hear the Italian heavyweight boxer Primo Carnera win the world title. Indirectly it was another triumph for the regime, but the sporting aspect was so much stronger than the political one that no one in the family – or indeed outside of it, so far as Irene could see – really noticed. Nonna Savia put cotton wool in her ears because the violence of the sport distressed her, Aunt Pussi did likewise, not on account of the violence but because, on a par with cycling, she held boxing to be common; everyone else, Lise and Tita included, not to mention Otto who was hoarse for a week afterwards, followed the match as if they were at the ringside – jumping up from their chairs, shaking their fists, waving their arms, shouting, cheering, gasping, and conveniently ignoring the fact that the broadcast was in relay and the result already known to them. Tommaso and Giorgio shouted louder than any one else, although Irene thought she heard Giorgio say something to Tommaso afterwards about sport being just another opiate of the masses. But anyway he said it very quietly and it was an opiate he appeared to relish.

Two days later there was yet another excitement and another gathering outdoors, in the hope – vain, as it turned out, but nobody minded, it was fun just looking – of discerning some trace in the sky or hearing some echo of the departure of the famous air squadrons led by the Fascist veteran Italo Balbo. Twenty-four planes flying all the way from Italy to Chicago and back again. The making of history, and again of a peaceful but at the same time debonair sort, because, as the news commentators pointed out, surely in good faith in this particular case, it was not a military enterprise the planes were involved in but a display of pure technology and Italian bravura. Fascism, after a dubious start, was showing its best and brightest feathers: it looked as if

Tommaso had been unnecessarily gloomy about what he called its 'essentially ruthless' nature.

Tommaso must have thought so himself, because in spite of the pressures of work he took longer holidays this year, and brought fewer books with him, and got into fewer arguments with the cousins. Irene was happier with him than she had ever been. She had always understood, from reading and hearsay, but particularly from reading, that, if you loved one person but were tied to another, the person you were tied to assumed hateful proportions in your mind. Or if not hateful then at any rate resentful, unsympathetic proportions: an unwanted partner was almost invariably portrayed as an unloved, unliked, and in some cases unbearable partner, often ending up in pieces in an acid-bath or trunk.

Nothing, she now discovered, could have less bearing on her own case than this casually acquired piece of information. In theory Tommaso might be the main obstacle to her happiness, and as such an object to resent, but in practice, especially now they had reached the fifth year of their marriage (eleventh year of the Fascist Era, as Renzino was instructed to date his schoolwork), he had become so much a part of her life as to make resentment impossible – she might as well resent the floor, or the air, or the force of gravity. His lovemaking, having passed the stage of furore when it had been so jarringly out of time with her own, now suited her perfectly once more: like a well-tried concert duo she and Tommaso had come to know one another's range, one another's repertory; they didn't always perform inspiredly but they never fell below a certain standard. And, as in the early days of their marriage, their coupling gave her in consequence a sense of rightness, of certitude, of things being in their proper place.

Their conversation had become practised too. They no longer discussed in the same depth the books they were reading, tending instead to pass them on to one another (or not, as the case might be) with a quick overall judgement like 'This you must read', 'This is not all it's cracked up to be', 'Don't bother about this, it's an utter waste of time', but nevertheless they seemed much better acquainted with what was going through the other's mind at any given moment. Anti-Fascism had become a bond between them – strictly speaking the first intellectual bond they had ever had – but they took it for granted, as if it had always been there, and in general talked less about politics and ideas, and more about their own concerns: the children, the dog, the family, fishing and other pastimes, and what they were going to do the next day. They took up tennis, playing gangly foursomes in the local club with Giorgio and Silvia. They played bridge (until they got good at it, when they became cross and competitive and had to give it up). They also discovered a growing mutual interest in food and cooking, and spent quite a large part of the summer together in the kitchen, inventing new dishes and creating what Assunta called *zizzania*, by which she meant fun and extra work, with the work predominating.

In fact they got on so well together that it occurred to Irene once or twice that the terms of the three-sided relationship could be expressed differently, and that there was an equally valid sense in which Giuliano, not Tommaso, might be said to form the obstacle to her happiness. At least in hypothetical terms. The happiness in question would have been less intense and doubtless there would have been less of it; nevertheless, without Giuliano to yearn for and eat her heart out over, it was a fairly safe bet that she would have been (reasonably? Tolerably? Who knows, perhaps even perfectly) happy in her present condition: married to Tommaso, rearing his children, doing everything that was expected of her and *only* what was expected of her, and in general housing, as Uncle Otto put it when describing his ideal of womanhood, 'no grasshoppers in her head'.

Unfortunately, though (or fortunately to Irene's way of thinking, who wouldn't have evicted them even if she could), the grasshoppers were there and continued to make themselves heard. Chirping louder and louder as the summer advanced until in the end she could hear no other noise, attend to no other message.

With the excuse of resuming her lessons she prepared for an early return to Florence, and Silvia followed suit, protesting with uncharacteristic frankness. All summer long her solidarity towards Irene had taken the form of silence – never a reference to Giuliano, never a question, never even a dig or a hint – but once the packing cases were out, almost as if affected by a tardy form of jealousy, her attitude began to change. Every time they were alone together she would corner Irene and accuse her, only half in jest, of the basest disloyalty towards herself and the children, dragging in the dog for good measure. 'This was *our* part of the year,' she would remind her. 'The best part – September and October, with the sun just the right heat and the beach all to ourselves, and sandwich lunches, and no husbands and no hurry and no fuss. And here you are, dragging us back to swelter in the city, all because of' – a gesture of her head towards the incriminated terrace – 'young Whatshisname over there. Oh yes, because don't think that I don't know your real reason for returning so early to Florence, Madamigella. Lessons, indeed! You have something *very* different in mind. Truly, Irene, your selfishness knows no bounds. You are a heartless mother. And a bad dog owner. And a worse sister-in-law. You ought to be ashamed of yourself, and I sincerely hope you are.'

No mention of Tommaso or being a bad wife to him, Irene noted, but even if there had been, Silvia's words would not have touched her. Shame, like temptation, lost its meaning once you disconnected it from wrongdoing. And she was *not*, repeat *not*, doing anything wrong. In fact, by Utilitarian standards she was actually doing right. The calculus was simple: at present there were three people, one of whom was happy and two of whom were desperately unhappy; whereas shortly there would be three people, two of whom would be wildly, unrestrainedly happy, and one of whom (provided the other two were careful) would be just as happy as before. Three in the place of one, an increase in happiness of two hundred per cent.

Excitement was so high in her that from the moment preparations for leaving began in earnest she started running a temperature. Morning sickness affected her as it had during pregnancy; her appetite dwindled to almost nothing. She was living off the energy of her own personal generator, which seemed from the throb of it to be located somewhere in the ventral region, between stomach and vagina, with repercussions on both.

Attuned to her movements, which he had been able to follow from his privileged position on the terrace, Giuliano telephoned only two days after her return to Florence. He rang towards evening, fortunately when Carmela was bathing the children and before Tommaso was back from work. He spoke so fast and so urgently that for a moment Irene had difficulty in recognizing his voice. He had found a place for them, he told her: the studio of a friend of his, a painter, or at least a would-be painter. Here was the address, she was to memorize it, on no account to write it down. The studio was on the very top floor of the building, under the roof, where the domestics' quarters used to be. They would both of them have to be careful about entering and leaving, because his friend's parents lived in the same block of apartments, and knew Giuliano's family well and probably Tommaso's also, so there was some danger of gossip, but apart from that the place was perfect. He could get the keys at a moment's notice, whenever he liked, whenever she liked. (A pause and a kind of strangling noise here.) But when *did* she like? Because he liked now, tonight. Or failing tonight, tomorrow morning. It was not emotional blackmail but he truly didn't think he could survive much longer than that: he had never wanted, never needed, anyone or anything so badly as he needed her.

The longing in his voice, approaching almost desperation, sent a wave of parallel longing through Irene's body. She felt sick, literally sick with desire to be with him, to be close to him, to annihilate the distance that separated them. 'Tomorrow morning,' she managed to say. 'I will be there tomorrow morning, as early as I can.' Then with shaking hands she replaced the receiver and stood empty-headed by the telephone, trying to fight off the nausea before joining Carmela and the children.

By the time Tommaso got back from work, an hour or so later, the sickness was vanquished and had been replaced by a kind of preternatural elation. Her faith might have deserted her but Irene had never felt herself so close to heaven. She hugged Giotto and Francesco rapturously as she put them to bed, hugged Carmela too, hugged the dog, then, having no one left to share her joy with, hugged herself as she lay in the bath, preparing her body for Giuliano and counting the hours that still had to pass before she could offer it to him. Only a few more to go, fourteen, fifteen at the most: why, oh why had she not opted earlier for this marvellously simple and marvellously satisfying solution?

Tommaso, when he came in, noticed her mood immediately and was infected by it. They were dining out that evening – with people he liked, not a business evening for once – and he sang a rude version of the Fascist marching song 'Giovinezza' as he changed his shirt, and made faces at Irene in the dressing-table mirror as she sat in front of it drying her hair (her preparations had been very complete).

Irene grimaced back, still exuberant, still on her personal cloud. Then, suddenly, something about the reflection of Tommaso's face in the mirror drained her elation away, leaving her in a state of total bewilderment. She saw him – well, how did she see him? It was a question she would often ask herself, and a sight she would often strive to recapture, usually in vain; she saw him as she had seen Giuliano, that was right. Just for an instant, a split-second, she saw him as she had seen Giuliano on the day of their first meeting: as a stranger, but a stranger who for some reason was infinitely important to her, infinitely precious. There was no time to make the thought explicit, but it passed through her mind that, if he had not been hers already, she would have wanted him every bit as urgently as she now wanted Giuliano. Possibly more so, because the face was somehow dearer and that much more compelling.

Later that night, and for many nights to come until it was so overworked it went dead on her, she was to pursue this line of reasoning consciously, deliberately, switching the poles of the status quo and imagining herself married to Giuliano (accustomed to Giuliano, sated with Giuliano, possibly bored with Giuliano), living in the other villa and staring backwards through the bougainvillaea at an unobtainable Tommaso on the other side. It was one of the few manoeuvres that brought any comfort. At present, however, seated at her dressing-table mirror, with the image of Tommaso already gone from it, already fading in her head, it was not reason that led her, it was panic. Bridge-burning, to be done at all, had to be done soon.

She turned round to face Tommaso. It *was* soon: so little time had passed that she could feel traces of the grimace still on her features. Which was wrong, but she could do nothing about it. 'I am in love with Giuliano Lessing,' she told him. 'I have been in love with him for over a year. What am I to do? Please help me.' A second later she could have bitten her tongue out, but the words were there, heavy and palpable as stones, and there was nothing to do but wait while they took their effect.

Her memory had another warp in it at this point (a convenient one in this case, she had to admit, so perhaps there was a little subconscious cheating involved), and of the long painful scene that followed, she never could remember very much: only the trappings, the inessentials, seemed to stick fast in her mind. Her hunger as the discussion prolonged itself past dinnertime and beyond. Her worries about what to say to Carmela and the friends they were meant to be having dinner with but now obviously weren't. Later worries about how to give Francesco his bottle, how to take the dog out, how, in short, to break the bubble of timelessness in which she and Tommaso were enclosed, without appearing callous or prosaic. They must have stayed there in the bedroom, talking, arguing, explaining, hurtling towards and away from one another like bumper-cars, until almost midnight, but apart from a Samson-like cry at one point from Tommaso – 'I have no weapons! A husband has no weapons by definition almost. How can I win you back without weapons?' – she couldn't remember a word either of them said. Nor what they did with themselves: whether they made love or kissed or embraced or even so much as touched one another. The chances were that they didn't, she thought, because the whole odyssey (when at last, defused, dehydrated, de-everythinged, they emerged from it) seemed not so much to have drawn them closer together as to have cleared a space between them in which they could not meet on different terms.

She remembered afterwards sitting down to bread and tomatoes in the kitchen, and trying not to equate the simple, wholesome, utterly predictable fare with her future life, and failing. And then laughing and telling Tommaso why she was laughing, and regretting it (his sense of humour had made strides but it still couldn't quite cope with this). She remembered also informing him, with her face turned towards the sink so as not to see his reaction, that she intended to go ahead and keep her appointment the next day with Giuliano, no matter what. Also the stinging of her eyes when she closed them in sleep, and the fear they would be puffy in the morning, and another inner laugh when she realized how vain in both senses this was. Little else. Perhaps, she sometimes thought to herself when trying to account for the lacunae, because the episode was another real watershed in her life, and water left very little trace.

CHAPTER XIII

On her way to the appointment with Giuliano next morning Irene felt the way she imagined a state executioner must feel: assigned to carry out a legalized action that was nevertheless unjust and cruel and intrinsically dirty. She had already discovered that morals had nothing to do with religion or belief in God, seeing that she had given up the one but seemed condemned to retain the other; now it seemed that they had little to do with logic either. How could an action be right and yet at the same time so palpably, distressingly wrong?

In view of the number of dress rehearsals that had preceded it, she couldn't help hoping, in a rather craven way, that the anguish of this umpteenth goodbye would be tempered by ridicule. You never knew, perhaps Guiliano wouldn't really believe she was serious about breaking her promise, perhaps he already didn't believe she was serious about keeping it. Or perhaps disappointment, and a well-founded suspicion of having been treated very badly, would make him angry. If it did, so much the better.

This hope was quickly shattered. Giuliano seemed to guess the purpose of Irene's visit immediately, even before she had entered the room, and to recognize the break this time as real and final and without appeal. He didn't show anger or surprise, wasn't even particularly curious about her motives; he just seemed, like herself, anxious to get the whole thing over with as soon as possible. This resigned attitude chilled Irene more deeply than any display of emotion would have done. When she began trying to explain things and begging him to understand and forgive, he simply put his finger to her lips, hushing her like a nanny, and told her not to worry, that these things didn't matter any more. The tone of his voice was not so much resigned, though, Irene now realized, as deadened: he spoke across a divide, as if one of them, it was unclear which, was already out of hearing.

They said very little after this, there was little to be said. Although they both knew that this was the last harvesting of their experiences together and that from now on they would have to live on their reserves, this particular experience didn't seem to be worth the gathering. With the politeness of a guide or an estate agent Giuliano led her round the studio, showing her his friend's paintings, pointing out the furnishings, making no comment save for a grim little nod at the bed, as much as to say, Well, there it was, if only we'd had a chance to make use of it. Then, holding his head very carefully, rather as if the neck muscles had been severed and he was obliged to balance it to keep it upright, he reaccompanied her to the door. Irene couldn't even bear to look at him properly: behind the façade of strength he seemed so vulnerable, so stricken.

On the threshold their reserve broke and they clung to one another, but only briefly, because physically too it seemed they could only do each other hurt by prolonging contact. All Irene managed to say as she let go of him, and this more as a statement than an apology, was, 'I am sorry I have given you so very little.' To which he replied, or she thought he replied (he spoke very quietly and she had already turned away, making for the stairs), 'I never said that you had given me little. I never said that at all.' Whether he closed the door behind her at this point, or whether he stood there in the doorway watching her until she was out of sight, she chose not to know. There was no noise whatsoever, and she did not look round.

As she made her way down the long dark flights of stairs – totally uncaring of the other residents, what did discovery matter to her now? – the thought passed through her mind, much as it had done during childbirth, that the pain was quite simply unbearable, but that if she did by some fluke manage to bear it, then in future she could bear anything. On a par with childbirth, it was the same low-centre part of her that ached, and when she reached the entrance hall she found herself inadvertently bending over and clutching herself there, like a soccer player struck in the crotch, and had to straighten up and compose herself before going out into the street. The pangs of love, she thought, so that is where they strike.

She walked slowly, aimlessly, relying on inertia for her direction. Almost as much as the parting itself, indeed in some ways even more so, she had been dreading the mid-morning return to the flat and the resumption of her routine: out with the dog, out with the children, what should they have for lunch, what should they have for supper, how should she find the time and the will to study. Normality wearied her, repelled her, almost frightened her. For a while at any rate she knew it would be her worst enemy: not suffering, not tears, not the kick-back of Tommaso's jealousy leading to further scenes, but the bland, smooth, unleavened normality of every day. In order to delay the moment of re-entry she was momentarily tempted to enter the Uffizi as she passed it on her way, but then realized that museums of any description would be off limits to her now, possibly for years, and trudged on.

When she reached home, however, there was a sensation, detectable even in the hallway, of things being slightly different from normal. The family was back, with all the clutter and confusion that that entailed, but she had known they were due back shortly and neither the return nor the confusion struck her as unusual. It was more the quality of the confusion: the maids' voices were lower, the aunts' and cousins' that much higher; the luggage was lighter and yet at the same time scruffier and looked as if it had been put together with more haste. Blacky, unattended by his mistress, wandered round the hall cocking his leg on the cases and getting in everyone's way; nobody shouted at him, nobody seemed to notice, not even the owners of the cases.

Nobody seemed anxious to acknowledge anything out of the ordinary either, greeting Irene with the usual shower of kisses and gossip and enquiries after the children, and it was not until lunchtime, when she called in at her father-in-law's flat to say hello to Nonna Savia and Renzino, that she realized what the matter was. Nonna Savia was dying, that was what constituted the dissonant element. Very unassumingly, very considerately, like she did everything else, Tommaso's grandmother was dying. At present it was only bronchitis – a touch of bronchitis as the other old people were careful to define it, *un pizzico, una puntina* – caught during the evening gossip sessions in the draughty hall of the villa, but from the flush on the old woman's cheeks and the weak, ineffectual sound of her coughing, Irene knew from the moment she set eyes on her that the infection was destined to worsen.

It would be misleading, and also false, to say, as Irene herself was sometimes tempted to in a mood of self-denigration, that she welcomed the idea of Nonna Savia's death or took any comfort from it. This was not so at all. Nevertheless she benefited from the death itself in several ways – not least because it gave her a plausible excuse over the coming weeks for the night-time tears she was unable to check – and in later years she would look back on it with a sense of gratitude, almost as if it had been a kind of parting gift from Nonna Savia to Tommaso and herself.

The most obvious benefit it brought her was quite simply occupation, the same dull but valid remedy as before. With what Aunt Frances called their 'earthiness' and she herself thought of as their sound, well-balanced attitude towards the flesh, she had somehow always expected the family to react practically in a crisis of this kind; instead they seemed to be disoriented, almost incapacitated by grief. Tommaso supervised the medical side of things, Silvia, flanked by Assunta and the other maids, took charge of the nursing, but when it came to sitting with the dying woman and keeping her company, neither of them showed themselves to be any more capable or willing than the rest, and by common consent the task fell almost exclusively to Irene.

This in turn brought her the benefit of a closer knowledge of Nonna Savia's character and vice versa. A deathbed was perhaps an unlikely place to strike up a friendship, nevertheless this was what happened: they became truly friends with one another. Almost accomplices. The tone, set not so much by Irene as by the older woman, started light and remained light for as long as lightness could be sustained: Irene sung snatches of opera on Nonna Savia's request, whose voice no longer obeyed her; she arranged her hair for her, brought her flowers and eau-de-Cologne; together they listened to plays on the radio – comedians, songs, whatever was going; they looked through fashion magazines and discussed the clothes. They entered into a kind of conspiracy, foreign to both, in which frivolity was the only virtue, gaiety the only goal. Paradoxically, but true to Nonna Savia's intent, it proved a very dignified way of dying: until the last, nobody was allowed to spoil things by looking sad or serious or worried, and the haemorrhage of grief which if unstaunched would have flooded everything, was stopped, as it were by a powder puff.

Yes, one way and another Irene discovered afterwards that she had a lot to be grateful for to Nonna Savia for these weeks of enforced respite from her own concerns. When it was all over, when the frail barrier of frivolity finally gave way under the reality of suffering, and the radio was switched off and the fashion magazines stowed away, and the other women of the family took Irene's place by the bedside (long faces didn't matter any more now that Nonna Savia couldn't see them), she allowed herself for the first time since their parting to go off on her own and cry – really cry, no fighting back the tears on Tommaso's account – for the loss of Giuliano. Only to realize that in the interim some kind of balm had mysteriously been applied to the wound, making the tears unnecessary. What was it Nonna Savia had said apropos love duets in opera? 'All that fuss about nothing. Heartaches indeed! I'd gladly sign on for some heartaches now.' Well, that, Irene supposed, just about summed it up: love, however painful, was a living concern, and as such she must learn not to grieve over it. *Punto e basta*. And now she must go back and try to comfort Aunt Lise, who was going to be the worst affected of all by the approaching tragedy, and try to persuade Silvia, who had been up all night, to get some sleep, and then go and pick up the oxygen cylinders from the shop to save Tommaso the journey, etc., etc. The end couldn't be far off now. Swift and hardly perceptible, like a mouse scampering across a floor, the unworthy thought flashed through her mind that perhaps Giuliano would come to the funeral and she would have a chance to see him one more time, perhaps even speak to him; but, just like a mouse, it was gone before she could do anything about it.

CHAPTER XIV

It must have been a time for watersheds and turning points, because Nonna Savia's death also constituted one as far as the family was concerned. Although its divisory structure didn't become visible for quite a few years.

Mercifully perhaps, because it signalled the beginning of the end of the old generation. The following spring, 1934, Aunt Lise, who had indeed been the worst affected by her sister-in-law's death and never really got over it, was run over by a car as she crossed the road. She had been on the way to visit her beloved Lutheran nuns, and they were the ones who picked her up and took her to hospital. She died in the ambulance. Her only concern, according to the nuns, was for the driver of the car and that no harm should come to him on her account. 'It was my fault,' she kept on repeating to them to the last. 'I dithered. It was my fault entirely, and that poor, kind man should not be dragged into it.' Irene had no use for saints any more, but this struck her nevertheless as a saintly way to die.

Otto lingered on another summer, regaining some of his old fire when Mussolini sent soldiers to the Brenner Pass in support of Austria, but otherwise broken by the loss of both sister and wife in such a short space of time. In November he had a heart attack in the bath, and another a few days later, just as he seemed to be over it, and died on the 8th – the day that Pirandello was awarded the Nobel Prize for Literature (which everyone agreed was a pity because in the generally glum panorama of European news it was the sort of item that would have appealed to him).

The unifying cross which he and Lise, Savia and Edmund, had formed, and which Irene had always pictured as a kind of knot (a real granny knot, she supposed) holding the family together, was thus untied, and perhaps as a result, or perhaps simply in line with the changing times, the whole structure of the family became a little looser, a little more ragged.

Otto and Lise's children, more prosperous now, moved out of the downstairs half of Aunt Pussi's villa and rented a summer residence of their own, much larger, and closer to the smarter Viareggio. Their move, far from being applauded, was looked on as an offence, and when they came to visit or to bring their young to play with their cousins (as they regularly did, being so close), they were treated with just a slight touch of ceremony – clean towels, instructions on how to reach the bathroom and so forth – to show that the offence had been pardoned but not forgotten.

Cousin Marco – more deviant still – developed a taste for the mountains as opposed to the sea and began taking Carla and children to holiday in the Dolomites for the month of August. Perplexing Aunt Tita, who never could make up her mind whether it was something to boast about – a son who could afford to eschew a perfectly good free seaside residence for a stay in a hotel – or something to lament.

Irene remembered Nonna Savia, in one of their last conversations together, pointing out to her, quite without acrimony, merely as an interesting fact to talk about, that the middle generation of the family was the least generous-hearted of the three. 'We were not good parents, you see,' she said, 'we were too soft. *Troppo dolci.* You never knew my daughter Lotte. She was a very good daughter, yes, a very good daughter, but she could have been better as a woman. I spoilt her, I never could say no, never deny her anything, and she grew up to expect too much. Like Lise's children, like Pussi's children, like Tita's children – good upright men and women but all takers; gobble, gobble, gobble, and hardly a thank you at the end of it. But *their* children, now they are a different matter – look at Tommaso, look at Silvia and Renzino, look at Monica and Guelfo and little Federico and the others. All big-hearted: the new generation are all givers again. Do you think this is the way it is, Irene, soft parents and hard children, and hard parents and soft children again, in layers like a cake?'

At the time Irene had laughed and said she hoped not, because that would mean Giotto and Francesco and Renzetto and Olivia were destined to be part of a tough layer, and she didn't like the thought of being squashed by them at all. As the seasons went by, however, she had to admit that Nonna Savia had summed up at least the middle group correctly, and that there was indeed a certain decline of kindness in this generation compared to the preceding.

Not that she was much affected by it personally: the only member of the new elder generation she had close everyday dealings with was her father-in-law Renzo, and he was gentle to the point of self-effacement and did not fit into the layer-pattern at all. No, it was more a question of the general atmosphere: with Savia and Lise and Otto gone, and Pussi following them in the spring of 1935, and only Tita left (minus Blacky and minus her cigarettes which she was longer allowed, and minus much of her old verve), the atmosphere of the villas and garden was no longer the same. The circle continued, but it was neither so large or so round as it had used to be; Assunta and one or two of her old cronies still sat there unperturbed amongst the *habituées*, but newcomers amongst the maids were not encouraged to follow their example, and when they did the other chairs would be just very slightly edged away from them, creating gaps and dents in the circumference. There were fewer chairs too: their maintenance had always been carried out regularly before, presumably under the supervision of Uncle Otto, but now nobody bothered, and when one broke it was carted off to the Fontana and left there to rot.

Irene didn't mind this change of atmosphere much either, or not as much as she might have done. It helped to underline a difference between eras, to allow her to look back on the preceding one with all that it contained and say, That part of my life, for good and for bad is over, let me get on with the next. She and Silvia, when they were not sunning on the roof, took to sitting in a corner of their own on the opposite side of the villa to the circle, earning themselves the new title of *le snobbone*, the snobs. From where they sat the Lessing villa was hidden behind a screen of acacias, and although this was not the real reason for her defection from the circle, Irene found she was more comfortable that way. Just as she was more comfortable *inside* the house now that she had swapped bedrooms with Silvia and no longer had the window to contend with.

Thanks to these and other small precautions, like changing her route to the beach and shopping early and sending Carmela to the kiosk for ice-creams in her place, in the two summers following their parting she barely caught sight of Giuliano at all. The first year nobody saw him, not even the attentive Monica, so Irene reckoned he must have carried out his original plan and spent the summer travelling. The second year she saw him twice, once on a boat with a crowd of other young men, once at the exit of the cinema, in the company of a thin blonde girl who Monica told her afterwards (very sadly) was an ambassador's daughter and reputedly his new fiancée. Both times Tommaso was with her and she could feel him silently pleading with her not to notice, and both times she turned away and pretended that she hadn't.

And that was all it had amounted to: two glimpses in two years. She refused to admit this, but Giuliano was receding slightly in her memory, occupying less floor-space. At nights she would think of him, but less and less spontaneously: sometimes only as compensation, after she had had a row with Tommaso, for example, or the children had been a nuisance, or her studies had been a grind.

In a way this was a relief, in a way it was just another, duller variety of pain. The effect on her marriage was positive, though, because she no longer felt any impatience towards Tommaso, nor was she tempted to cast either him or the children in the role of prison warders; she just, as she seemed to remember Aunt Frances had once instructed her to do, put her head down over her bicycle bars and pedalled. And discovered to her satisfaction, as she kept it up, that she was eventually getting somewhere.

In the autumn of 1935, however, her steady course was

interrupted, through no real fault of her own. It was the time of Mussolini's invasion of Ethiopia. The summer had already seen a build-up of colonizing zeal, even in the family itself, and there had been several tiffs with the cousins about what they called Eden's 'interference' in the Duce's perfectly reasonable plans to gain an empire for Italy. What was wrong with an empire, after all? they would ask, singling out Irene as their special target. Hadn't any country worth its salt the right to an empire? And who was England to criticize when she'd conquered half the world? Envy, that was what it was. *La perfida Albione* changing the rules half-way through the game to prevent anyone else from getting a look in. Nobody in this family had ever championed Mussolini and they weren't going to start now, but in this case they were sorry to say he was in the right, and it was England, Irene's England, that was behaving badly. Besides, Ethiopia was a backward country, and there was still slavery and injustice there, and Italy could do a lot of good by colonizing – build schools and roads and things and institute proper law courts and introduce the locals to the joys of the cinema. Why, the paper said that most of the population was clamouring for Italian intervention, there had been pictures of soldiers being welcomed with flowers. One man had even been given the present of a lion cub: he had it in his arms, you could see it, it was sweet.

This sort of thing went on, good-naturedly but with growing annoyance on Irene's part (who found the empire argument very difficult to answer without sounding unpatriotic), all through the summer. Normally she and Silvia would have had their usual peaceful weeks alone in the villa in which to unwind and relax and forget all the friction, but this year was Renzetto's first year at school and they had to return early to Florence. There were pinafores and satchels and things to be bought, perhaps even (although Silvia thought she could get round this with doctors' certificates and a bit of wangling) an ugly little black Figlio della Lupa uniform, to be worn for Saturday drill. Renzetto, predictably, was longing to don one of these.

They left Forte dei Marmi on the last day of September. Three days later the invasion proper of Ethiopia began, and ten days later the League of Nations agreed to impose sanctions on Italy as a result. (Under great pressure, of course, from the ever more perfidious *Albione*.) The family made no snide remarks this time to Irene, in fact their loyalty was aroused and they drew closer to her in order to protect her from possible insult, but the general mood of the Florentines was angry. Irene found a card pushed through the mailbox with the words '*Bottana Inglese*' written on it (spelt wrongly: the correct word for whore was *puttana*). One of her regular tradesmen – the butcher – refused to serve her, others kept her waiting and served her only when they had to. Meeting Aunt Frances in Doney's for a coffee, a man from a neighbouring table, when he heard them speaking in English, leapt up and snatched the sugar from them, saying, 'Now you learn to do without it too,' or something of the sort.

It was nothing really, but coming after a summer of persistent needling on the subject it was enough to unsettle her, and in complete agreement with Tommaso, who was anxious above all for the children to be spared any nastiness that might come their way, Irene decided to return with them to Forte until things had calmed down a bit. There was no danger on the sentimental front: the Lessing young were always punctual schoolgoers and the villa had been shut days before Irene and Silvia left.

The villa had been shut, and was still shut when Irene and Carmela arrived and began re-opening on their own account. In the later afternoon, however, when Irene, relaxed and windblown, wandered back from the beach with the children along the usual path, one of the windows on the ground floor was open and she heard music coming from it: somebody was playing a radio or a gramophone.

The sound, signifying in itself very little – it could have been the caretaker, it could have been the Admiral on the run, it could have been anybody – acted on her defences like the trumpet of Joshua, shaking them to their very foundations. She knew, somehow, with groundless but absolute certainty, that it was Giuliano, and she knew also that, smother them though she might, deny them though she might, her feelings towards him hadn't really changed. The old yearning was still there, ready to break out in fever-force if given a fraction of a chance.

That night she moved back to her own room and took up her position by the window, wallowing in this small transgression like a reformed drinker off on a secretive binge. She left the light off, so as not to betray her presence, but when, as she was certain she would, she heard the sound of footsteps on the Lessing stairway and saw the lone figure of Giuliano come out on to the terrace with a gas-lamp in his hand, she could not resist emitting some kind of signal, even though she knew it was foolish of her, and gave a loud cough and then a sort of throat-clearing noise, just to see how he would react.

He reacted wonderfully and badly, depending on how you looked at it, and Irene looked at it both ways. He leapt, literally leapt to attention, like a hare on hearing hounds; the gas-lamp slithered from his grasp and he caught it automatically at knee-level without lowering his head from its alert position. By the light of the flame as he lifted it again, Irene could see that every inch of his body was tense with the effort of listening. She gave another cough and he whipped round to face her in the darkness, but turned away just as quickly when he saw the closed shutters, and extinguished the lamp with an angry gesture and made off down the stairs again. Then the gramophone started up as before: Caruso, Irene thought it must be, in some Neapolitan song she had never heard – very sad, very beautiful. Oho, she thought, with a flare-up of happiness idiotic in the circumstances, so that is the way things are with him too: ambassador's daughter and all, that is the way things are with him too.

She stayed by the window until Caruso's voice was silent and she heard the sound of closing shutters in its place. The cold night air must have sobered her up a bit, because when she went to bed the resident band of grasshoppers, who had been getting horribly out of hand and chirping all sorts of wild instructions – Go to him. Knock on the shutters. Spend just one night. Just one hour. No one will see, no one will know. Don't you think you owe him something after what you have done to him? Etc., etc. – were a shade more subdued. Nevertheless she knew she was in for a long and restless night. It was a relapse, and a bad one.

Next morning she woke up very early – or got up very early, she wasn't sure she had really slept at all – and began packing. Thankfully it was raining, and neither Carmela nor the children were likely to kick up any fuss when she told them of her change of plans. Her emotions were numerous and muddled, and later she knew she would have to sort them out, but at present she could feel only exasperation: exasperation with herself, with the situation, with the time and effort she appeared to have wasted utterly, seeing that after nearly two years of struggle she was back in square one again. Even exasperation with Giuliano. Or perhaps especially with Giuliano. Because what was he doing there, all on his own in Forte dei Marmi at this time of year? Surely it wasn't normal for a young man of – what was he? She still didn't know his age, twenty-five? Twenty-four? Perhaps even younger – to hole himself up in a deserted seaside villa in the off season and listen to records? (No, to *a* record, because it was always the same one that he played.) The chances were that his solitude had nothing to do with herself, and he was simply studying for his finals or something quite legitimate like that, but even so he cut a melancholy, almost heart-rending figure.

Back in Florence, she tried to dismiss the whole episode from her mind – cancel it out as if it had never happened. This worked fairly well in the daytime, but at night she started having a recurrent dream, the symbolism of which was so crude and so naïve that its meaning was impossible to ignore. She would dream that she and Tommaso had left the villa at Forte dei Marmi, as they did every autumn, having shut everything, tidied everything, put everything away, and were driving back to Florence (which by dramatic licence was confused in the dream with England and lay on the other side of the channel, three days' journey away). When they reached the outskirts of the city she would suddenly panic and realize that someone or something had been left behind, and begin checking and counting cases and shrieking the children's names, only to realize that the missing element was the dog, and that she had shut him on the Lessing terrace, with nothing to eat, and nothing to drink but seawater.

The third time she had the dream she got up, even though it was the middle of the night, went into the sitting-room (with the same sweaty, guilty feeling she had had in the days of the midnight telephoning), and wrote Giuliano a letter which she posted the next day without re-reading. It was the classic, rather smug, rather schoolmarmy 'I hope all is well with you because I am fine' sort of message, in which she explained that the whole story between them had, from her point of view, been nothing more than a regrettable mistake, due to youth and inexperience and an over-fertile imagination. Now that she was older she had come to realize that the only man she really loved was her husband, that this had always been the case, even when it had seemed to her that it hadn't, that she wished Giuliano the same fortune in finding a partner, etc., etc., etc.

The text repelled her, so did the thought of Giuliano's reaction on reading it. Nevertheless she knew it was the best and most generous leaving present she could ever hope to give him. The only thing that remotely comforted her was the logic behind the gift: rather like the riddle of the Cretans, if what she said was true, and she never had loved Giuliano, then it was necessary that he receive this letter in order to regain his freedom; if on the other hand the text was false and she had loved him and still did, then it was *pari passu* necessary that he receive this letter – in order to regain his freedom. Which hypothesis was correct was something she need not bother to find out, seeing that both arrows pointed in the same direction: send, send, send.

She neither expected nor received an answer, but a reward of a kind soon came her way, because the dreams stopped immediately, and shortly after Christmas Monica informed her (not sad this time but furious) that Giuliano was unofficially engaged to the ambassador's daughter and that Signora Lessing and the Admiral were dancing hornpipes of joy.

CHAPTER XV

Another question people would sometimes put to Irene in later years, although not until the war was long over and the subject had lost its embarrassment value, was about organized Fascist violence. Meaning the squads, the intimidation, the beatings up and castor-oil dosings and so forth. What had it consisted of, they would ask, for someone in her position? Had she ever suffered it? Had anyone in the family ever been touched by it? Had she ever observed it close to?

It was a question she always found very difficult to answer truthfully without giving a totally false impression of the way things had been. Strict adherence to the facts seemed almost necessarily to commit her to the jocular, and Fascism had been no joke. Not for the multitude of ill-equipped, ill-informed soldiers who had died for it; not for the Jews who had been deported to concentration camps on account of it; not for the political prisoners and the resistance fighters whose lives and liberties had been sacrificed in the struggle to overthrow it; not for the ranks of an increasingly hungry, bewildered and betrayed civil population. Not even for people like her or Tommaso for that matter, or Silvia or Giorgio, or Aunt Frances or her friends, or anyone who seriously dissented from the regime.

And yet, perhaps because her own life was so sheltered, perhaps because that side of things was over by then and Fascism had become respectable, or perhaps simply because she was lucky, Irene could remember witnessing only one scene in any way connected with the type of violence the questioners had in mind, and that was when, on her way to the market on New Year's Eve to buy lentils which the maid had forgotten, she caught sight of a group of callow spotty youths in uniform, strutting along the pavement towards her, chanting the anti-British ditty of the moment, their genitals cupped insolently in their hands to make their meaning clearer. '*Sanzionami* QUESTO, *Albione rapace, Lo so che ti piace, ma non te lo do.*' Sanction THIS, greedy Albion! I know you like it, but you're not getting any from me! Whether these were indeed members of the infamous Squadracce, as an old man beside her whispered in fright, and whether their insults were meant for her or just coincidence, were two things that she never really found out, because seconds later the tension of the scene collapsed in best comic-opera tradition, as a ground-floor window flew open and a woman leant out of it with a carving-knife in her hand and shouted, '*Sporcaccioni*!' You dirty louts! 'Come over here and I'll sanction the lot of you!' causing all the passers-by to burst into laughter.

To the strains of this anti-sanctionist song (which Tommaso found irresistibly funny and used sometimes to sing to Irene with a wicked leer on his face before they made love), and the equally catchy and in some ways still more vulgar 'Faccetta Nera', Pretty Little Black Face, the new year, 1936, got under way. It was the year of warfare, sanctions, autarky, national pride and national touchiness, of belt-tightening and buying Italian. And *speaking* Italian, and wearing Italian, and eating Italian, and doing everything in the most Italian way that could be contrived or imagined. The streets were full of advertisements for Italian wool-substitute – Lanital – made out of milk residue. ('Don't wear it if you're holding a baby,' quipped a comedian on the radio, 'or you'll find yourself ending up in your underwear.') Shop windows displayed patriotically produced scents, guaranteed free of Parisian influence: Parma Violet, Alpine Lavender, bottles of cloudy Venetian toilet water – said by the sceptics to come straight from the canal. The papers gave counsels on how to get round using French and English words: drink *ristretto* in place of consommé, wear a *maglione* instead of a pullover, stop taking the ferry-boat and start travelling by *pontone* like Julius Caesar did when he invented mobile bridges, and on the subject of bridges, give up bridge and begin playing *ponte.* Some suggestions were so hilarious they could only have sprung from irony on the part of the journalists: *code di gallo* instead of cocktails, for example, or *dieccis* instead of tennis.

It was also the year of a terrible polio scare which kept all parents of young children in almost constant alarm throughout the summer, of the outbreak of the Spanish Civil War which stencilled the divide between right and left and strained family relations even further, of Hitler's visit to Rome and a parade of swastikas that made everyone's flesh creep when it was shown on the newsreels (could it be that something worse than communism had sneaked into the world?), but in spite of all these things it went down in Irene's memories as a curiously happy period. The Giuliano episode she looked on (with regrets, but tender, bearable ones) as finished. She knew, from catching sight of him occasionally on the beach or the terrace and observing the way his head jerked round at the sound of her voice or the calling of her name, that she was still present in his thoughts despite everything, but the knowledge was no longer essential to her: it touched her, even pleased her, but she could have done without it. Perhaps done better without it.

Her marriage to Tommaso, on the other hand, struck her not only as not finished but as just beginning: in the sense that the years of shared experience seemed to have turned them both into two quite different people united by quite a different relationship. From nothing but physical attraction, not always very well distributed, they now had virtually everything in common – the same feelings, the same aspirations, the same worries, the same children (who were often the source of the worries: in July, when Francesco ran a fever, they sat up with him for three days and three nights without cease, watching for signs of the dreaded paralysis), the same likes and dislikes, the same habits. Lots of shared memories as well, funny and sad and mixed. Lots of pooled knowledge. Lots of simple ballast. Life did not stretch out in front of them full of promise – the times were already too hectic, too uncertain; it presented itself more like a helter-skelter track, full of dips and bends and unseen hazards. But whatever it offered and whatever it consisted in, Irene felt that she and Tommaso were better equipped than most couples to complete the course in maximum harmony. So perhaps in her last message to Giuliano she had written the truth: after all, what did they know of one another really? And if love depended on knowledge, as the course of her marriage seemed to indicate, what love could be said to exist between them? Giuliano had thought her capable of speaking to her child like a dog; Tommaso knew that if anything the reverse was true and she was more inclined to speak to her dog as if he were a child.

In the summer session she passed her state exams and qualified for university. The family by and large found it faintly inelegant – this desire on the part of one of their female members to continue studying (only women who weren't properly provided for and needed to find jobs did that) – and hardly bothered to congratulate her on her achievement. But Tommaso reacted wonderfully, even showing a certain amount of pique at her high marks, and made a big fuss and took her out to dinner in Florence with Silvia and Giorgio and the classics coach, and Aunt Frances came too, and they managed to order proper champagne and drank it in defiance of the sanctions, and all in all Irene felt very pleased with herself and her powers of stamina. Six months later she knew she probably wouldn't remember any Greek at all, and the Latin would be all tangled up with the Italian, but that wasn't the point: the point was that her bicycle had passed another hump from which there was no backsliding.

In the autumn Giotto started school. Even though it was a private school, and Renzetto and Olivia were there already and seemed to be coming to no harm, Irene had been dreading on Giotto's behalf the impact of the Fascist educational system: the bias, the bombast, the militaristic emphasis. The teacher he was assigned to, however, turned out to be a woman of over fifty, commonsensical and kind, and so old-fashioned in her methods as to be practically untouched by recent directives. 'I am afraid I don't hold with these new textbooks,' she admitted almost apologetically to Irene at their first meeting, 'nor with all this drill and gymnastics nonsense. I like my children to sit quietly in the classroom and learn to read and write and do their sums the way their parents did. *Pinocchio* has served me quite well as a reader for generations of pupils and I do not intend to change now. I like them to wear their little pinafores and bows, too – more comfortable. And as for exercise, there is the play-break, which gives them quite enough opportunity for playing soldiers. If you are dissatisfied, of course, you can always ask for your son to be transferred to another class – to that of Maestro Codebò, for example, who has much more up-to-date notions.'

Irene was not dissatisfied and did not transfer Giotto to Maestro Codebò, but left him thankfully where he was – with Collodi and the values of the nineteenth century. On rally days and Fascist commemorations, when uniform was required for teachers and pupils alike, she followed Silvia's example and produced a certificate from the family doctor to say that her son suffered from *ginocchio valgo*, whatever that was, and was unfit to take part in the assembly. There were never any questions asked. One day Giotto returned home in high spirits, saying he had seen the *negretto* and been allowed to touch him to see if the black came off, and she and Tommaso, on further enquiry, discovered that an officer from the Ethiopian Army had been led into the classroom and put on display there (he was apparently touring all the schools in the region, poor man, on orders of the Ministry of Education). But this was the only concession to war-propaganda that the teacher ever made, and since the introduction of the officer appeared to have been made in a friendly spirit, and permission to touch had come from him, Irene quelled her indignation and said nothing, and persuaded Tommaso to do the same.

Shortly after Christmas she and Tommaso went skiing in the Tuscan mountains with Silvia and Giorgio, leaving all four children behind in the care of their grandfather. It was the first real holiday they had ever taken, and they were determined to enjoy themselves and did. For two weeks nobody mentioned the names of Hitler or Franco or Mussolini, or remarked on the sinister drawing together of the three dictators, or listened to the wireless, or even bought a paper. They just battled in the snow, all four of them, with their straps and boots and sticks and sealskins, and concentrated on techniques for governing the seemingly ungovernable planks of wood to which their feet were tenuously attached.

Skiing was thought by those who didn't practise it to be an elitist sport, and on their departure the cousins had made ironic remarks – 'Look at our four champions of the working classes!' 'Oh, but they're not going for the enjoyment, they're practising for Siberia!' 'Watch out or you'll find yourselves bumping into the Ciano set!' and so on. In actual fact, as Irene soon discovered, it was a pastime for the mountain-mad and other lunatics, in which category she happily belonged. There were no ski-lifts, no runs, no waterproof clothing, very few instructors, most of them improvised and interested only in acquiring new drinking companions and making their female pupils fall down so that they could pick them up again. In a day, if you were lucky, you could manage three brief and hazardous descents; the rest of the time was spent clambering and sweating and putting your skis on and off and digging yourself out of snowdrifts. Nobody in the post-war years was able to believe her when she said that it was fun, but it was: it was superb, one of the happiest holidays she ever spent.

When she got back to Florence she realized that she hadn't thought of Giuliano once during the entire fortnight. She was cured: the mountains had cured her, as they were reputed to cure sufferers from tuberculosis. In the past she had always thought that if any terrible catastrophe took place – if war broke out, or the Black Death returned, or the end of the world came – she would grab the children and the dog and flee to Giuliano, wherever he was, and spend her last days with him. It had been a kind of test which she applied to herself (and also a kind of mawkish fantasy in which she indulged: he and she together at last, Mr and Mrs Robinson Crusoe, in a disintegrating world, beyond care, beyond values). Now even this last hypothetical thread was broken, and she knew that, in an extreme situation, although she might still veer towards Giuliano in her imagination, it would be Tommaso who she would cling to in the flesh.

With the coming of the new year she buckled down to her university syllabus. The King's love affair with Mrs Simpson, presented in the Italian press with great sympathy as the romance of the century, seemed to have softened everybody's hearts towards England, and she met with no gibes from her fellow students on account of her nationality. (Personally she didn't find the story very romantic, but she feared that this was just high-mindedness on her part, or else plain envy for two people who, unlike herself, had placed passion before everything.) The outside world seemed to be set on a threatening, disorderly course, but in her own little planetary system everything was at last relatively harmonious and tidy.

CHAPTER XVI

This state of outward disorder and inner peace continued for months, increasing on both fronts. Mussolini sent troops to Spain in support of Franco. Giorgio, in one of the most dramatic Sunday lunches ever, announced to a horrified family that he was going too, to fight on the other side. (In fact he got as far as San Remo and then came back again, a bunch of carnations in his hand for Silvia, having developed shingles in the train.) The Pope came out with his encyclical letter against Hitler, which rattled the family badly because it evidently meant that the German dictator *was* as evil as he was made out to be after all. Gramsci died in prison, which rattled them less – dangerous communist *agitatore* that the man was. Guernica was destroyed. The Roselli brothers, two socialist exiles whom Tommaso greatly admired, were assassinated in France, somewhere near Alençon. To Aunt Frances's especial dismay, English newspapers, which had never been either abundant or punctual but had filtered through none the less, were suddenly banned. What was more the family car, now virtually Tommaso's car, because Renzo stayed more and more at home and hardly used it any longer, had its tyres slit as it stood outside the laboratory, and the letters 'NON FI', meaning nobody was quite sure what, but probably *Non finisce qui*, This is only the start, written on its bonnet in red paint. Nobody discovered who did it or why, it was just another symbol of the times, as senseless as it was sinister. There was no precise awareness of standing on the rim of an abyss, because that was the sort of knowledge that came only with hindsight, but there was a sense of instability in the air, and, rather as they had at the time of her infatuation with Giuliano (she thought of it as infatuation now, or tried to), Irene's spirits would soar and plummet with each bit of good or bad news. Things are going to be all right, no they aren't, yes they are, no they aren't – until she began to feel her stomach was attached to a Yo-Yo.

In the midst of all this, and perhaps to some extent as an unconscious reaction against it, the core of her existence remained extraordinarily peaceful. She attended her lectures, studied hard whenever she could, walked the dog, took Francesco to the park, ferried the elder children to and from school when it was her turn, took them to swimming lessons and fancy-dress parties, went out to dinner with friends, went to restaurants, went to the cinema, did all the things she had done before, and more, but with a new sense of serenity. It was, after all, her life: not a cage any more but a structure, more like scaffolding or a climbing frame. Silvia, who to start with had been a bit resentful of the time Irene dedicated to her studies, forgave her and their friendship continued as close as before: the rift was still there but they had become practised in ignoring it, it wasn't much wider than a hair's breadth anyway. Apart from the chores like chauffering, which they divided on a rational basis, they did nearly everything connected with the children together, in a seldom silent, mostly screaming sixsome – seven with the dog. This too, in its paradoxical way, was peace.

The summer started out in much the same pattern: international affairs were perhaps a tiny bit calmer, Irene's own affairs, thanks to a drastic, head-on, eye-to-eye meeting with Giuliano at the gate of the villa the moment she arrived, which made her fear another relapse, a tiny bit rougher. But that was all. The weather was magnificent, the children free and untroublesome, and so happy to be where they were that their happiness was infectious. Tommaso, after a long struggle with his conscience (was it right, when it cost what one of his workers earned in a month?), bought a boat – a small fishing dinghy with a sail and an inboard motor, and a ladder which could be lowered into the sea for bathing – and their beach lives improved dramatically in consequence. Better fishing, better swimming; diving, which no one had been able to do before, except from off the float of a *pedalo*; visits to other beaches (or other stretches of the same beach, but even so it made a change). Also, as Silvia and Irene were quick to discover, magnificent sun-bathing, far superior to lying on a scalding roof with nothing but a pail of water to cool off in.

They got into the habit of skipping the family lunch, and during the early hours of the afternoon, when the children were resting, they would return to the beach with a thermos and a couple of sandwiches, anchor the boat a little way off the shore, and lie there basking like lizards, plopping in and out of the water at intervals and dozing and talking of nothing in particular, until the children reappeared with Carmela and demanded their attention. Irene's study books, which she brought with her as a sop to her conscience but seldom opened, became stained with sun-oil and seawater – marks of her indolence and contentment which much later on, when she took up the books again in very different circumstances, would awaken in her an almost unbearable sense of nostalgia.

The texture and pace of life in the villas had altered now almost beyond recognition, and Irene was aware that she and Silvia were partly responsible for the change. With their desertion of the lunch table the midday meal had become a scrappier and more informal affair. Renzo was still served a proper three-course meal in the dining room, even on weekdays, but the children usually preferred to eat in the kitchen with Carmela and the maids, and Renzino, following the bad example of his sister and sister-in-law, often didn't turn up at all but stayed on the beach until late afternoon and stuffed himself with left-overs when he got back. Assunta, at first disoriented but quick to see the advantages, began laying on a different type of cuisine – less pasta and less fried foods, more bread and salads and *salame*. Once upon a time this would have been a disgrace, a declaration of defeat; now she appeared to regard it more as a declaration of independence.

Dressing habits had also changed. By the time Irene and Silvia got back from the beach with the children there seemed little point in putting on smart afternoon clothes just to sit in the garden for an hour or two, and they took to staying in their bathing suits until it was time to dress for supper. Sometimes, if they weren't going out to the cinema or anything, they would hardly bother to do even that, and would come to table in cotton sarongs tied hastily over their costumes, and with the children already in their nightgear. Renzo blinked but said nothing: female fashions were beyond his powers of assessment.

Less dressing up meant less washing and ironing, and fewer get-togethers in the Fontana for the maids. Which again brought advantages and disadvantages to those concerned, the former greatly outweighing the latter. Everyone had more time and lighter duties, and everyone knew it and was grateful. Everyone, not only Irene and Silvia in their sarongs and the children in their sandals, also had far more freedom. And yet in some strange way the tempo of life itself seemed to have speeded up, so that the days, instead of longer, seemed to have grown shorter. Making a nonsense of the benefits, because what was the use of double the leisure time if it passed twice as quickly? The 'five o'clock' trolley seldom made its appearance in the garden: the brewing of tea had become too much trouble, and you couldn't get tea anyway, you could only get something called Carcadè, or Karkadè, which was imported from Egypt. As Assunta was wont to say, laying the lone place for her employer at the head of the table, or sitting in the kitchen with her feet up, staring at her rusting frying pans, '*Stavamo meglio quando stavamo peggio*.' We were better off when we were worse off.

In a sense Irene and Silvia both agreed with her and felt guilty about their innovations, but not to the extent of giving up their lazy sunny afternoons or donning silk dresses and stockings to sit around and sip the occasional cup of Carcadè, or Karkadè. In fact as the summer advanced and the heat increased they stayed longer and longer at the beach, sometimes coming back only an hour or so before supper.

One evening they stayed particularly late, and instead of returning by the longer route (which Irene was still careful to take so as to avoid any further unsettling encounters with Giuliano), they took the shorter one through the pine wood, emerging right in front of the gate of the Lessing villa.

Neither of them paid much attention nowadays to the neighbouring household, but it was immediately apparent, both to her and to Silvia, that something unusual was taking place inside. The gate was wide open and two powerful, military-looking motor cycles stood in the drive. On the terrace the figure of the Admiral could be seen, standing, not sitting as was his habit at this time of evening, talking to two strange men in the uniform of the Carabinieri, also standing. He was waving his arms about and appeared, even from a distance, to be in a state of extreme agitation.

'Do you think the vice squad has caught up with them at last?' Silvia said. She didn't normally appreciate Giorgio's witticisms, but his fantasy about the Lessings' scandalous private lives was one she couldn't resist. 'I bet that's what's happened. What else could it be? Unless the Admiral had been gun-running for the Republicans or one of the boys has nicked a car.'

Irene laughed, but already something about the figures of the Carabinieri on the terrace – their gestures, the awkwardness of the way they stood – told her that their errand was a serious one. Joking aside, illegal action on the part of any member of the family was out of the question, so what did that leave? Mutiny on one of the Admiral's ships? An accident to one of his men? To one of his relatives? To one of his children?

She would have liked to go straight inside to her lookout post at the window (Silvia's window now) and see if she couldn't discover more about what was going on from there, but the moment she and Silvia entered the garden of the villa they were waylaid by Eva, who had special visitors she wanted them to meet, and drawn into the ring of the knitting circle. Irene managed to find a chair from which she could keep an eye on the comings and goings on the Lessing terrace, but what with making conversation to the guests and answering questions and showing off the children and trying to prevent the dog from leaping into people's laps, it was very difficult to read any sense into the scene. It was growing darker too, which didn't help matters.

The Carabinieri left almost immediately, the moment Irene was seated, but the Admiral did not accompany them, nor even, as far as she could make out, say goodbye. Instead he turned his back on the two men rather rudely and crossed over to the edge of the terrace where he stood standing staring out over the pines for what must have been a full two or three minutes, perhaps longer. Then he disappeared inside the house and the terrace remained deserted. The garden too, which was unusual for the early evening, when the children were normally at their rowdiest and the ping-pong table and football in constant use. Shortly after his disappearance, a window on the same floor was thrown open and then slammed shut again, and then another one on the floor above.

Irene was distinctly worried now and found it difficult to concentrate on what was being said to her. The next figure to appear on the terrace (although there may have been others which she missed: she couldn't look all the time) was the old maid, the one who spat on the ironing. In the normal course of events it was her task at this point of the day to tidy up and fold the newspapers and light the lamps and the mosquito coil, and generally prepare for the Admiral and Signora's after-dinner relax. This evening she performed none of her habitual tasks, merely picked up one of the cats, which she was usually the first to chase away, and did a slow dance with it, round and round in a stately waltz rhythm, then put it gently down and covered her head with her apron. She looked to Irene to have gone quite batty. But then the whole household looked odd. Where were they all? Why was everything so quiet?

When at last, with the excuse of Giotto's and Francesco's bathtime, Irene was able to make her escape from the circle and take up her position at the window, it was almost dark. She was convinced now that her first hunch had been right and something, if not grave, at least very serious had happened: the Lessing parents were such methodical people; in all the time she had observed them (and how closely she had observed them) they had never varied their schedule in this way.

She began running through again in her mind the possible alternatives, coming to the reluctant conclusion that the only explanation that accounted for both the visit of the Carabinieri and the strange immobility that followed it was that of an accident. Presumably to some member of the family, not merely an acquaintance, and presumably fatal, because otherwise there would have been uproar, not this terrible, brooding silence. She was desperately trying to prevent her mind from going any further along this line of reasoning when she saw in the half-light another figure emerge on to the terrace. It was Signora Lessing herself.

For a few seconds Irene's fears melted away to nothing and she found herself smiling alongside with relief: Signora Lessing without any further ado plumped herself down in one of the deck chairs – not the one she normally sat in, another one, but this small variation of place did not seem very significant – and began laughing. Her well-groomed white head rocked back and forth, becoming less well-groomed by the second, her shoulders shook, her entire frame heaved up and down, she appeared literally to be convulsed by mirth. Irene went on watching and smiling, until her eyes grew adapted to the evening light and were able to pick out more details; then, with a feeling of absolute disgust at herself for being so stupid, she realized that the woman was not laughing at all but crying. Crying as she had never seen anybody cry, never thought possible that anyone *could* cry.

Was it then that she guessed the truth? Rationally speaking it should not have been then, but a few moments later, when, shifting her gaze to the far end of the Lessing garden, she spotted Giuliano's younger brother Umberto, crouching in the shadows by the side of the water butt with a stone in his hand, systematically smashing to pieces the goggles and the cache of Roman remains – clunk! clunk! clunk! – as if he were trying to punish them, which probably he was. That should have been the moment the truth hit her. Or else a little later on when another larger group of Carabinieri arrived with their burden; unmistakable, even though it was covered by a length of dark-blue cloth – a tarpaulin, or perhaps one of the officer's cloaks.

Reason, though, works slower than other faculties of the mind, and in her memory – whenever she allowed her memory to tread this ground, which she seldom did – Irene identified the moment of her own awareness of loss with that of the grotesque spectacle of the laughing/crying mother. It could have been any son, any daughter, the Lessings had so many; and yet somehow she knew immediately, the moment her mind made the switch from, This is laughter I am watching, to, This is grief, that it was Giuliano who Signora Lessing was grieving over.

The same ugly instant of awareness should also have seen the beginning of her own grief, but since much of her mourning for Giuliano had from a practical point of view been done already, its starting point was a little more complicated. Also its course. Also, inevitably, its management. Standing there by the window, watching the homecoming of her lover-that-never-was, unable to move, still partially under the anaesthetic of shock, one of her first explicit thoughts was connected with power. I can deal with this, she thought. If I have held out so far, when another option was always there, always open to me, always beckoning, then I can hold out now when the option is no more. It seemed a solid datum, something to latch on to and use as a prop. She was soon to discover, however, that in the realm of true bereavement things were not so simple, and that Nonna Savia had been right when she made light of sentimental heartaches. They *were* light in comparison, they were like piffling little tufts of thistledown.

CHAPTER XVII

It was like a physical wound really, Irene supposed. Imagine you had sustained a wound that you were unable to dress, unable to medicate, unable even to acknowledge. In the foot, say, or the arm or the hand. (No, the foot, definitely the foot, because that was where it was eventually to make itself felt.) Imagine yourself walking on this open wound every day, hiding it by a boot so that no one could see it, but walking on it, running on it, jumping on it, never allowing anyone to suspect that it was there. How long would it take a wound like this to heal? How painful would the process be, and how messy?

She put it like this, of course, in rational terms, much later on, but even at the time she knew that this was not the way to go about recovery. The trouble was, though, that she had no choice.

On the evening of Giuliano's death she was able to cry. Everybody cried – Monica, Assunta, Carmela, Aunt Tita, the children, even the gardener. Crying was not only in order it was *di rigore*, that is, it was pretty well obligatory. Since the lamented was young and beautiful and lived so close, crying could even be extended to howling: it was good neighbourly behaviour, no more.

It was also good neighbourly behaviour to attend the funeral two days later, but this Irene could not bring herself to do. Tears at the moment of tragedy were one thing, tears which continued to flow unchecked for twenty-four hours and beyond were another, and she could not trust herself to appear in public without showing something more than the amount of sorrow that was expected of her, not even when screened by the barrier of her dark glasses which she had donned on the evening of the accident and scarcely removed since.

It was a Saturday, the first Saturday in August, and the day that Tommaso closed down the laboratory and began his summer holidays. He arrived while the funeral was in progress. Not the best-chosen of moments, it seemed to Irene, but at least it meant that he and she were able to have a little time together, more or less in private, in which to talk and adapt themselves to the new situation. The villa was nearly empty: everyone, except for Aunt Tita and the children, had dressed up in their soberest holiday clothes and gone to church.

Irene had given little thought as yet to Tommaso's reactions, being too taken up by her own, but instinctively, as she did in all things now, she counted on his support. The moment she saw him, however, or perhaps it would be more exact to say the moment he saw her, she realized she would have to do without it and manage on her own.

'Take your glasses off,' was one of the first things he said. Then, almost angrily, after he had taken a look at her eyes, 'No, put them on again!' Her grief he accepted as inevitable – over the telephone the previous evening, he had even, in a touchingly clumsy way, tried to share it – but its actual manifestation, now that he was obliged to take notice of it, seemed to distress him beyond his powers of control.

They left the children in the care of Aunt Tita, or vice versa, and went down to the beach. 'Cry,' he said, holding her close. 'Get it out of your system.' But as with the glasses, no sooner had she obeyed him than he sharply countermanded the order. 'Not like *that* for goodness sake! Surely you don't have to cry like that?'

His disgust at her tears had little or nothing to do with public opinion, Irene soon realized; it was a private, internal matter. He was torn between generosity and jealousy, between genuine concern for her sadness and a kind of necessary blindness towards it. He appeared to be asking her to confide in him and let him comfort her, but really all he wanted (all he could bear?) was for her to tell him that little or no comfort was needed.

For ten minutes or so after this outburst, generosity got the upper hand and he spoke to her with real tenderness and understanding, even going so far as to admit his conviction that Giuliano, to have conquered this place in her heart, must have been a very special person. 'There is a saying in Italy,' he told her, 'which goes like this: "The friends of my friends, are my friends." I believe this is nonsense as regards friendship – think of some of the people we've met through our own friends at dinner parties – but I think it holds good for love: the people who are loved by those we love, I mean, are people that we ourselves – in different circumstances maybe – would or could have loved. I am sure I would have loved your Giuliano, Irene – if I had known him, and if he hadn't been your Giuliano.'

After this almost super-human admission, though, which made Irene want to cry even more, the pendulum of his jealousy swung back again, and he began watching her like a hawk for further signs of what he evidently considered despite himself to be her worst betrayal yet. Irene could feel his attention on her like a weight.

'You feel better now?'

'Mmm, I feel a bit better.'

'You feel like a swim?'

The place Giuliano had drowned, caught in a fishing net while diving for his *anforae*, was about half a mile away, on the same beach. To Irene the whole stretch of water was hateful, hostile. 'No, I don't think so, not today.'

'It's very hot, though.'

'Yes, you're right, it is. Perhaps later, when Silvia and Giorgio get back.'

'OK, later then. There's a good film on tonight, by the way.' Then, drawing very close and lifting the glasses, 'Or don't you feel like going to the cinema either?'

No, she managed to say reassuringly with a smile, the cinema would be fine, but did she have to decide right now? Couldn't it wait till later?

Eventually she compromised: the beach with no bathing,

just watching the others, and the tennis club instead of the cinema.

This last proved a great mistake. Or perhaps, as she came to think a little later on, there was no mistake about it but the fulfilment of a definite plan. There was a tournament on, and the clubhouse was filled with people and music. There was no chance of playing, all the courts were taken over by the competitors, but there were a couple of matches that Tommaso and Giorgio and Silvia wanted to see, so they sat in the stands, all four of them, watching until well after midnight.

In Irene's case, without seeing anything. The moment they were seated, someone, she never discovered who, began playing with manic regularity, time after time, until she was surprised no one got up and demanded a change of tune, the Caruso record which Giuliano had played that autumn evening as she had watched him unseen from the window.

Tommaso's attention was on the game, and Irene still had her dark glasses on: she felt she could safely give rein to her misery. The aftermath of tears posed no problem, her eyelids seemed to have reached a stage of saturation, they didn't get any less puffy but they didn't get any more puffy either. (A condition which was to last so long and look so weird that she was finally obliged to take Silvia's advice and pass it off for public purposes as an allergy to mascara.) Behind her lenses, against the backdrop of blood-red courts and white lines and white dots and white shapes, all mingled up and running together in a dreadful, streaky, bacon-like effect, she wept and wept and wept, catching the tears on her tongue and swallowing them down tidily, out of sight. And the more she wept, the louder and more insistent became the tenor's voice in her ears, until she gradually became convinced, in spite of knowing that it was irrational and foolish and possibly rather unbalanced of her to harbour such a thought, that it contained a message for her from Giuliano.

'What is this song?' she whispered to Silvia, when it started up for the fifth time.

'I know, isn't it awful,' Silvia said. 'You'd think they'd have something a bit more up to date, wouldn't you? It's a famous old Neapolitan song, "Fenesta che lucive". It's getting on my nerves.'

'What does it say? What do the words say?'

Silvia looked a bit cagey and took refuge in vagueness, which perhaps was authentic. 'I can't really hear them all that clearly,' she replied. 'Something about a window that used to have a light in it but doesn't any more. Probably it's to do with broken hearts or death – they nearly all are. *Not* very appropriate for you in your present state. Do you want me to go and ask them to change it?'

Irene shook her head, and the tears escaped sideways, a good inch off the drinking course. Hastily she wiped them away before Tommaso could see them. She knew she would have to investigate the song further one day, when she felt strong enough, but in the meantime Silvia's brief description gave her all the proof she needed. A song about a window, addressed to a window. It was just as she thought: Giuliano was trying to get in touch with her. He had used the song before to try to get through to her, announce his presence, make her listen to him, and he was using it now. How such a thing was possible was something she didn't care to enquire into too closely, conflicting as it did with her dismissive views on the afterlife and the immortality of the soul, but she presumed there must be some physical cause which presently defied explanation. Perhaps, who could tell, in a case like this where death was premature and sudden, part of the mind lived on on its own for a little while like the tail of a lizard? Perhaps energy remained? Perhaps the will? Anyway, the mechanics didn't interest her: the undeniable, tangible, all too audible fact was that Giuliano wanted to communicate with her from beyond the grave and had somehow achieved this end.

In all the song was played nine times, five times running and four more at intervals (which ruled out coincidence: no tune had ever been played in the club that often in a single evening), and was still wafting across the courts when the match ended and Tommaso suggested, an element of test still in his voice, that they wind up the evening by eating ice-creams.

'I think the kiosk will be shut by now,' Irene said, careful not to worry him by an outright refusal.

'Ah, but they've got some on sale in the clubhouse. I already asked.'

'Then that would be lovely.'

'You're sure? You're not feeling sick or anything?'

She felt so sick that the prospect, the word, the concept of ice-cream made her stomach turn. She knew that she would have to pretend to eat the stuff and then get rid of it somehow when Tommaso wasn't looking.

'No, why should I be?'

'Well, then, what are we waiting for? Ice-cream for everyone. Chocolate, vanilla, whipped cream, the works!'

Test, scrutiny, compliance on her part and relief on his – it was the pattern to which nearly all their exchanges were to conform for quite some time, sex included. A few days later there was the question of the visit of condolence to be paid to the Lessing family. Irene knew that the visit would be an awkward one – unseemly if anyone in the family knew of her liaison with Giuliano, meaningless if they didn't, and difficult to carry off in either case – and yet for some strange reason she found herself desperately longing to go. Merely, she supposed, in order to hear his name mentioned, be in the company of people who had been close to him, see the rooms in which he had lived. There was no way of explaining this to Tommaso, however, and in answer to his careless (but oh, so careful), 'You weren't thinking of either of us going, Irene, were you?' she could only answer, 'No, I wasn't thinking of either of us going. Why? Do you think we should?'

'Not particularly, not unless we want to.' A pause. 'But perhaps you *do* want to.'

'Of course I don't want to.'

'Are you sure? When Papà asked who was going to accompany him, I thought I saw you – '

'Saw me what?'

'Nothing. I thought you looked as if you wanted to go, that's all.'

'But I don't want to go.'

'No, I know, you've just said so. But all the same you think you should?'

'I didn't say I thought I should, I said I thought *we* should. No, I didn't even say that, I asked *you* if you thought we should.'

'Why did you ask, though, if you didn't want to go?'

'I didn't ask, I just wondered. It was you who brought the matter up.'

'So you don't want to go?'

'No, I don't want to go.'

'You really don't?'

'I really don't.'

'Well, that's settled then. Neither of us goes.'

'Yes, that's settled. Neither of us goes.'

Like the smothering of her grief, the swapping of such complicated insincerities between them seemed to Irene, even then, a bad sort of habit to slip into, but once again there was no apparent way of avoiding it.

CHAPTER XVIII

Irene was ignorant of the workings of the psyche, in those days most people were. When, a few weeks later, the pain that would hit her every morning on awakening like a retarded whiplash was replaced by tiredness and lethargy, she took it as a good sign. She stopped dreaming of Giuliano, indeed she virtually stopped dreaming: this was a good sign too. She had no desire to talk about him, no desire to think about him: *um so besser* (as Aunt Tita would sometimes say, in one of the few German locutions that she still remembered). It was less of a good sign that she could no longer summon any interest in her studies, and didn't want to read, and on Carmela's day off could scarcely bother to dress the children, but there you were, tiredness was tiredness, and if you were too tired to do one thing, you were too tired to do another. Otherwise it was called laziness, and Irene knew she wasn't lazy, she was just desperately, desperately tired.

Their seaside life had become so simplified and easy-going that for the time being this lethargy of hers went more or less unnoticed. Silvia would sometimes give her a worried, faintly puzzled look and ask her if she was sleeping properly; Tommaso, fastidious about such things despite his proletarian sympathies, would sometimes point out to her that her nails needed varnishing or that the hairs on her legs needed attention, to which she would reply with a noncommittal, 'Mmm, so they do,' thinking to herself that she'd just as soon sweep the sand from the beach as pick up a nail-file or a pair of tweezers, but that was as far as it went; nobody else seemed to notice there was anything amiss.

When they returned to the flat in Florence, however, the seriousness of her condition began inevitably to make itself felt. First of all to the children, who became impatient with her slowness and sluggishness and always being told 'later', or 'tomorrow', or 'when I feel like it', and then to poor Carmela, who found herself saddled with more and more work. Irene did everything she *had* to do (which, once she'd ruled out study and dog walks and the hairdresser, wasn't very much), but day by day the effort became greater. In the afternoons, when it was Silvia's turn to accompany the children to their tennis lessons or piano teacher or wherever they were going, she started taking to her bed, where she would lie immobile for longer and longer periods, curled up on her side like a foetus, staring at the wall. Sometimes the dog, although increasingly restless from lack of exercise, would consent to lie there with her, and when it did she would hold it close and twist the hairs on its back between her fingers, working them into kind of miniature hayricks. For some reason this pastime gave her a great sense of peace.

Less so the dog, however, and when, as it regularly did after five minutes or so of passivity, it rebelled or wriggled away, she would transfer her attention to her feet instead. At first treating them gently, as she did the dog-fur, but gradually increasing the pressure and driving her nails deeper and deeper into the skin – the hard part, the part on which she walked – until by the end of a month of such treatment she had created a series of deep, raw weals, not painful enough to prevent her from walking, but painful enough to oblige her to walk with a limp.

Tommaso, when he questioned her about it and discovered what she had been doing, was more helpful than she thought he would be. He must have known that the self-mutilation was connected in some way to Giuliano's death – in a dull, brute way she knew it herself – but as long as the connection was not explicit he seemed to be able to deal with things rationally and calmly.

'You need a doctor,' he said. 'Not just any sort of doctor, a special sort of doctor. I'll see if I can't find somebody suitable.

In the meanwhile keep your stockings on, even in bed, and cut those dratted fingernails. You'll be all right, I promise you, you'll be all right.'

The web of insincerities they had spun for themselves being several layers thick by now, Irene half-feared he would send her to a chiropodist. His understanding of her plight, however, was evidently much greater than he cared to admit. Two days later he came back from work with a visiting card in his hand: 'Dr M. Löwenstein, *Specialista in Malattie Nervose*'.

'The man has no telephone,' he said, 'so you'll have to call round and see him for your appointment. He lives quite close, so I think you'll make it if you start out early.' (Her lack of energy, undisguisable now, he had decided to treat as a joke.) 'I'm told he's very good.'

'For feet?'

'For everything.'

Dr Löwenstein not only had no telephone, he had no furniture either. When he opened the door to Irene's ring she thought for a moment she must have come to the wrong address. (She asked him about this later, when she got to know him better, and he gave her the eye-opening and, to someone in her state, very salutary reply, 'I had a few pieces with me when I arrived, *cara* Irene, but work was scarce and I was obliged to burn them in order to keep warm.') It didn't take her long to realize, however, that the address was the right one and Dr Löwenstein, indigent and furnitureless though he was, was the right doctor.

His qualifications were many, far more than appeared on the card: he could have approached her case in a number of ways. He could have dismissed the feet as irrelevant and gone straight to the head; he could have taken his cue from herself and Tommaso and concentrated on the feet alone; he could have made a compromise and baptized her complaint 'nervous mycosis' or something similar, and prescribed a long course of applications of special anti-mycotic lotion and got her to talk to him while he applied it (which, for Tommaso's benefit, was more or less what he did). Instead he appealed to her heart and her intelligence – and to her sense of mischief. 'There is nothing wrong with you, young woman,' he told her after a brief but thorough examination. 'Nothing that time will not cure far better than I can. There is, on the other hand, a lot wrong with me. Your husband is rich, and kind, and worried, and willing to spend quite a lot of money on your account. I am – I make no secret of it – desperate, I cannot afford to turn away such a promising patient. I suggest therefore you come here twice-weekly, during your afternoon rest-hour for preference, which seems to be the worst time for those poor, abused feet of yours, and submit to an entirely illusory course of treatment, the cost of which will enable me to keep – what is the English saying? – body and soul together, the wolf from the door. What you do while you are here is your affair, but I have a great liking for your countrymen's habit of drinking tea round about that time of the day. If you agree to my rather mercenary but candid suggestion, perhaps you would be so good as to bring some with you. Also a kettle. Also some cups and saucers. I think I can provide the spoons.'

He was taking a risk, of course, but as he told Irene afterwards, if she was clever then it was the best way of getting her to talk to him in the leisurely, uninhibited way that he required, and if she wasn't clever then he didn't really want to talk to her for very long anyway, despite the fees.

And he did talk to her. He was, as she later discovered, a famous exponent of the Freudian method of psychoanalysis, in which the patient is meant to do all the talking and the therapist the listening, but, perhaps because he sensed that full analysis was unnecessary, or perhaps because he knew already that time was scarce (or perhaps truly because his need was greater than hers), his approach from the start was that of simple, and indeed at times rather one-sided, conversation – a friend talking with a friend. A *talkative* friend talking with a friend.

Not only non-Freudian, it was in effect the old, antithetical, Christian remedy of forgetting the self in order to find it. However, although applied by a declared pro-Freudian and anti-Christian, it appeared to work. These twice-weekly hours of conversation – at first a duty (just as Dr Löwenstein intended), then something a little less and a little more and a little different – gradually became one of the most important features of Irene's life: the hinges on which the closed door in her mind was finally able to turn. For the first time since Giuliano's death she found herself with something to look forward to. Dr Löwenstein was neither young, nor attractive, nor happy – in fact, with his lean, furry appearance, and cunning, hunted eyes, he reminded Irene of some outsize rodent, driven from its rightful environment and trying to survive on its wits – but he was without exception the most interesting person she had ever come across. There was not a continent, not a country almost, he hadn't been in at some time or another, not a language or a culture he wasn't familiar with to some extent. And whereas in most people such knowledge would have produced superficial certainties in him, on the contrary, it appeared to have instilled profound and deeply meditated doubts, which he seemed willing, indeed anxious, to discuss with her.

Aunt Frances's tea-line was still mysteriously open: of champagne and newspapers there was no longer a trace, but the Earl Grey tea continued to arrive through its former privileged channels. Irene went to see her over Christmas and begged several packets which she took along with her to her appointments, to Dr Löwenstein's delight. 'It is one of life's paradoxes, maybe,' he said, sniffing the steam from his cup like a cocaine addict, 'but the fact is, luxuries are essential when you have nothing. In profusion, mediocrity goes unnoticed; in a void, only the best will do. I am afraid my flat, if ever I set about it, will prove very difficult to furnish.'

By the time the university re-opened after the Christmas vacation, Irene was well enough and bright enough (and sound enough) to contemplate attending lectures. She expected Dr Löwenstein – Maurice, as she now called him – to encourage her in this, but he surprised her by doing quite the opposite.

'I would tread carefully if I were you,' he said, 'on those newly healed soles of yours. It is no good taking something up if you are shortly to abandon it.'

Irene was rather hurt by his lack of faith in her staying powers. She had told him very little about the affair with

Giuliano – he had asked her very little; nevertheless she thought she had made clear to him that will-power had not been lacking on her side, if anything the reverse.

'But I have no intention of abandoning my studies,' she objected.

'Intentions don't come into it, *mia cara*,' he replied softly. 'We have been talking these past weeks about everything that lies under the sun. What we have not talked about is the future that lies under shadow. You are foreign, your children are half-foreign, your husband is a brave man but he holds unpopular views, I am told several of his employees are bitterly critical of his management: events may force you to give up your studies, and much sooner than you think. *Pardon*, than *I* think: from your face I see this line of thought is new to you.'

This was not quite exact: until lassitude had taken over, Irene had worried a good deal about the future. She knew what Maurice meant, though: neither she nor Tommaso had anything approaching his sensitivity to danger, his readiness for flight. In one of their earlier conversations he had asked her, perhaps as a delicate character-probe, what things she would take with her if her house were to catch fire (people were excluded, presumed already safe), and she had replied after a moment's thought: her dog, her jewellery and her photograph album. When she had put the same question to him, he had replied with no hesitation at all: his passport. At the time the answer had seemed to her disappointing and somewhat incomprehensible: a passport, surely, was something you could always get replaced? Now she began to understand the significance behind their different priorities. She and Tommaso had lived the largest part of their lives in a world they could, broadly speaking, trust. Maurice, in contrast, was familiar from the cradle with the kind of world that their own world was turning into, or perhaps had already turned into: a world where rights were precarious and power was capricious, and a passport photograph of oneself more important than a photograph of home or friends or family.

From that day onward the tenor of their conversations

began to change. Before, as Maurice had pointed out, they had veered towards sunny topics. (And why not, when the aim on both sides had been principally to cheer?) Now they stepped, more or less voluntarily and yet with the uncanny propulsion of outside events, into darker areas altogether. Austria was Maurice's homeland, or the closest place to a homeland he had ever known, inasmuch as he had been born there and had lived there for the first eleven years of his life. In February the country came prominently into the news. The Chancellor, Schuschnigg, after a meeting with Hitler, the climate of which was hard to reconstruct from the Italian press but evident from the results, released all the National Socialist political prisoners and appointed as ministers three sympathizers with the formerly outlawed party. It was, according to Maurice, the end of Austria's independence and the beginning of full-scale European conflict. 'Your English government's policy of appeasement is lunacy, Irene. How do you appease the appetite of a ravenous tiger? Simple: by feeding it every day with bigger and bigger morsels. And that is what they are doing. The Rhinelands for breakfast, Austria for lunch, who knows? – Belgium, Denmark – for tea, France for supper. And then what? The next day the hunger will still be there. Stronger than before because the stomach will meanwhile have grown larger.'

Except for by a couple of old fogeys at Aunt Frances's when she had gone to collect the tea, Irene had never heard canvassed this terrifying idea that there might shortly be war in Europe. Tommaso's predictions were grim and growing daily grimmer, but they were on a smaller scale: he was worried above all about Italy and Fascism, and tended to judge events in other countries according to the effects they would have on the regime. The appointment of Seyss-Inquart and the other two Austrian ministers was bad: it strengthened National Socialism, and therefore it strengthened Fascism. This, and the contrary view adopted by almost everybody else (that it was a good thing and weakened communism), was the way in which most people's minds in Italy seemed to work.

Maurice appeared to view the matter in an altogether deeper

and more disquieting perspective. 'The Jews I meet here do not want to listen to me, Irene,' he confided to her urgently one day over the rim of his teacup. 'Why should they? I am a renegade, an outcast with few friends and no money and no influence whatsoever, my Italian is not even all that good. But I am telling you, in Germany Jews are already being *killed* on account of the fact that they are Jews. Not imprisoned, not forced into exile (although that is happening too), but *killed*. This is the truth. I will not tell you how I know it, because it would undo all the work I have done and you would start tormenting your feet again, but I assure you it is what is taking place. A murderer has come to power in Europe, and he will not stop with the Jews. Nor will he be content with my beloved Austria.'

Events over the next few months seemed to prove Maurice right. In England Anthony Eden (that *gorgeous* young man with all the right ideas, as Aunt Frances called him) resigned office, precisely over the appeasement question. His place was taken by the allegedly more accommodating Lord Halifax (Lord Shilly-shallifax in Aunt Frances's lexicon). In Austria things rapidly went from bad to worse: Schuschnigg was forced to abandon the Chancellorship and the pro-Nazi Seyss-Inquart was called on to form an interim government, the first act of which was to invite the German troops into the country in order to 'help restore order'. It was, as Maurice had foreseen, the end of Austrian independence. What he had not foreseen, however (and when he did see it, it reduced him to tears), was that ninety-nine point seventy-three per cent of his countrymen or quasi-countrymen would declare themselves in an April plebiscite to be in favour of the take-over. In Czechoslovakia a similar sort of mood amongst the German-speaking part of the population seemed to be in the air. With Maurice to spell out the meanings of each new development, Irene began to live in a state of almost constant anxiety.

From a strictly personal point of view the anxiety was positive. It drew her out of herself, in a straight uncomplicated line towards Tommaso and the children. Maurice, whom she had now begun to confide in (when she could: he was such a talker himself that it was none too easy), encouraged her to tell him about Giuliano, but more often than not she found she didn't want to – not out of reticence but because she had other more pressing matters on her mind. What to do in the event of war. Whether to remain in Italy or to return to England. How to convince Tommaso to leave his family, his work, his homeland and everything that was dear to him. In the event they did decide to leave, whether to try to convince Silvia and Giorgio and the children to come with them. How long to wait before deciding? She had used to speculate before on who she would fly to in a moment of world catastrophe, Tommaso or Giuliano. The choice was no longer open to her, but now, with the catastrophe at hand, she tested herself again in a purely academic way: Tommaso, she would want to be with Tommaso.

'Why?' Maurice asked her when she told him the result of the test.

She thought carefully, you had to think carefully with Maurice. 'Because I like his smell,' she replied, somewhat to her own surprise. 'Because I feel at home with him.'

Maurice nodded. He didn't look surprised at all. 'Did you not like the smell of the other young man?'

She thought back: the meetings between Giuliano and herself belonged to the cold season, there had nearly always been overcoats and scarves between them; only in Torre del Lago had she caught the full flavour of his person – his skin, his sweat, his spittle. 'I did, yes I did,' she said slowly. 'But it was stranger, harsher. If I had ever lived with him I think I would have to have taught him to wash more often and change his shaving lotion.' As she said this she realized it was the first even remotely critical thought she had had about Giuliano since his death. She wondered if the fact was of any importance.

'What you say there is very important,' Maurice commented, as if reading the question inside her head. 'It shows that this business has at least taught you something about love. Love is protean, amorphous. We are the ones who channel it and force it to take shape and direction. Stop thinking about it in terms of Newtonian physics: more here, less there, block that stream and the other will flow stronger. That is the way we make it work, not the way it works itself. You loved the other man, you still do; if he had lived you might have grown to love him very much. In which case you might have had to make adjustments, dig different channels, build and dam and scurry around like a beaver. As things stand, however, it is your husband who you love and will love and have loved all along, and nothing needs doing about this at all. Go on cherishing your other love for as long as you want to or need to, go on missing it, go on mourning it: your love for your husband will not suffer or grow any smaller as a result.'

'You are sure of this, Maurice?'

'As sure as I am about anything. Which is not very much. But, no, I am sure.'

'Then why should Tommaso mind so much – about my crying? Couldn't you explain to him? Couldn't you stop him minding?'

'The problem is not with Tommaso, Irene, it is with yourself. *You* stop minding for a start. Tommaso's troubles we can deal with later, when he starts limping or trying to turn the dog into a porcupine. And now to more serious business. Have you heard about the visit? Have you seen the preparations? I came to this city to lose sight of the *Hakencreuz*, the hooked cross of Nazism, and here it is, on my very doorway almost. Don't say you haven't noticed. Put your head out of the window a moment. Take a look, take a look. And then shut it again please and draw the curtain.'

CHAPTER XIX

The decision was not an easy one to come to, in fact Irene was never really sure when or how they came to it or who came to it first, but at some moment during that troubled spring of 1938 she and Tommaso made up their minds: they would leave Italy for England with the children should the international situation get any worse, with a view to seeking permanent abode once they were inside the country, and in the meantime they would ready themselves for departure.

For someone of Tommaso's background the decision, or the tranquil acceptance of such a decision, was so extraordinary as to convince Irene even further of its rightness. She had always expected him to resist like a mandrake the uprooting from his native soil, but on the contrary he seemed almost to welcome it: Italy, as he put it to her simply, was not a place he wanted his children to grow up in any more. True, he made endless attempts over the coming months to convince Renzo and the others to follow his example, but in the face of their refusals never once did she hear him say, Then I'm not going either, or anything of this kind. (Which was lucky, because she didn't like to say so but the man at the Consulate had been explaining their position to her and she feared it was going to be hard enough gaining asylum for the four of them, let alone for half a dozen of Tommaso's relations.) She realized what pressure he must be under, both at work and at home, and how little she had done to ease this pressure and how much to increase it. The thought saddened her, but it even crossed her mind that his curious readiness to quit his homeland might be connected in some way to her affair with Giuliano: who knows? Perhaps he sensed that it was still not properly resolved, and wanted a new start for them both, in a place without reminders. Without ghosts.

In ridding them of their last shreds of doubt, the conversations with Maurice were a powerful influence, of course. So was Hitler's visit and the fuss and the flowers and the cheering that accompanied it (and which no amount of curtain-pulling could conceal). So was a full-scale family row that developed some days after the visit, in which all the menfolk with the exception of Giorgio and Renzino turned against Tommaso and accused him of bringing disaster on their house by his failure, as they put it, to resign himself with *buon senso* to the inevitable. None of them had been in person to watch the festivities, but the local cinema had already shown several newsreels of the event, and the arrogant bearing of the German dictator, plus the offhand, elder-brotherly way in which he treated the Duce (until yesterday his mentor), seemed to have depressed them all dreadfully.

Although impressed was perhaps closer to the truth. Renzo, so accustomed to his timidity as to be unashamed of it, even managed (quietly) to admit as much. 'Of course I am impressed,' he whispered to Irene when he was sure Tommaso wasn't listening. 'Power is always impressive; your Mr Chamberlain understands this very well. Did you see the way Hitler treated the Duce? Condescending to him, patting him on the head almost. It used to be a meeting of equals, with Mussolini if anything cutting the better figure – remember that mackintosh, how drab it looked beside the Duce's uniform? – but there's no doubt now about who's boss.'

This, spoken or unspoken, seemed to be more or less the opinion of everybody, and even though the splitting of the clan was an event of unparalleled gravity for them – far worse than the original exodus from Germany which was now simply a part of their history – no member of the family seriously intervened to hinder it. It was as if they all recognized in their heart of hearts that, for this potentially vulnerable branch of their tree, lopping it off and transplanting it in safer soil was the best solution. Alone with Irene, Silvia would occasionally give in to despair and would burst into tears and cling round her neck and beg her to reconsider and remain. 'If war really breaks out you may *never* come back. Anything may happen. It may last for years, and our children will grow up strangers to each other, going to different schools, speaking different languages. They may not even recognize one another if they cross in the street, think how terrible that would be.' But punctually after each outburst, and just as Irene had begun to waver, she would stiffen up again and assert that no, it was all for the best, and of course they must go, she was just being selfish and stupid – not to mention trite: *how* Giorgio would tease if he'd heard her uttering that banality about the street-crossing! – and Irene wasn't to listen to a word she said.

Assunta, too, when she was informed of its likelihood, kept up an ambivalent attitude towards the departure, sometimes weeping and tearing at her hair in the grand peasant style, sometimes railing against Mussolini for the mess he had landed them all in, sometimes (more often, to tell the truth) mumbling just loud enough to be heard the chauvinist proverb '*Moglie e buoi dai paesi tuoi*', A man should choose his wife and cattle from his own village, implying that the mess was not so much Mussolini's fault as Irene's for being English and Tommaso's for marrying her. Carmela, who in the event of their leaving had agreed to stay on to look after Renzetto and Olivia, said and did nothing at all, neither to mourn nor to blame, merely looked stunned, as if someone had cuffed her repeatedly about the head without cause.

Apart from these three exceptions, however, everyone else did their stoical best to make the coming separation as painless and undramatic as possible: it was in the children's interest, it wouldn't last long, things would blow over and they would soon all be reunited. And besides, nothing was definite yet, they still had the summer in front of them, and the summer might bring about all sorts of changes in the world scene; there was no point putting the wagon before the oxen. Aunt Tita, still lucid behind her trembling façade (she was slowly succumbing to Parkinson's Disease), was almost girlishly enthusiastic about the move. Aunt Frances likewise. She had half a mind to join them, she told Irene excitedly over the telephone, in fact she almost certainly would sooner or later; the only reason she still hesitated was that her flat had recently been put under observation by the Carabinieri – 'On account of the *salotto*, you know, which they see as quite a little hot-bed of conspiracy' – and she was afraid her departure would be construed as giving in to the brutes. Although, she added quickly, to be quite honest, the Maresciallo in charge was not a brute at all but an absolute sweetie-pie, and popped in for tea and biscuits all the time and they were getting along famously, so Irene was not to worry.

Irene didn't worry, or not about Aunt Frances anyway: it sounded as if political persecution was agreeing with her and she was having her first real fun in years. She worried, however, about almost everyone and everything else. Passports, tickets, permits, affidavits, quarantine regulations for the dog; Carmela, the family *in toto*, the friends she and Tommaso would leave behind – Maurice in particular, what, oh what would become of Maurice? The flat, the furniture, the plants and who would water them. The children and the effect that this upheaval would have on them. Tommaso and the same, compounded by the anxiety about what he would do for a job if the move became permanent, and whether in the event of war he would end up in an internment camp like his grandfather had, branded as an undesirable alien: Wop or Kraut or possibly in his case both.

The summer, which was to have provided them all with a last, poignant taste of family peace and togetherness, was similarly peppered with upsets and worries. In June all four of the children developed measles and then passed it on to poor Giorgio (who was in fact extremely ill with it, although never quite ill enough for dignity to conquer over ridicule). Irene, who had hoped to be able to return to Florence now and again for a meeting with Maurice, was marooned, irritably, among the thermometers and camomile poultices. The patients itched and thrashed in the heat, and she itched with them and for them: poor little Olivia was so badly affected that her hands had to be tied behind her back to prevent her from tearing the skin off her face. There was never any real cause for alarm but it was a worrying, difficult time altogether. Irene sat in Nonna Savia's old bedroom, transformed into a hospital ward for the occasion, reading and telling stories until her voice gave out, and combating on her own account an at times irresistible urge, in this climate of fretfulness and forbidden scratching, to return to her habit of feet-peeling.

After the measles, and perhaps on account of the weakness the measles produced, came an outbreak of nits, which again started with the children but did not confine itself to the children. Of dignity this time for the adult victims, not even the shadow. The cure consisted in dousing the head with liquid paraffin and wrapping it for a period of at least seventy-two hours in a headscarf to do away with what were politely called the *bestioline*; after which shampooing could proceed, followed by a thorough, manual, hair-by-hair pick-through – monkey fashion – in order to remove the eggs.

For the females, even fastidious ones like Carla and Eva, the first part of the business could be managed quite suavely: headscarves, tied jauntily in a bow on the top of the head in couturier style, were all the fashion, and provided a bathing cap was worn underneath to conceal the smell of paraffin and block the escape routes there was no reason why the carrier of the expiring *bestioline* shouldn't go around as if nothing had happened, even to church. The males, on the other hand, especially the older ones, looked undisguisably grotesque under their turbans – like landbound pirates or ugly old fortune-tellers – and on Carla's orders were confined to the house while the paraffin phase lasted. They weren't even allowed to sit in the hall, for fear the delivery boys would catch sight of them. Irene, surreptitiously, made sketches of them all, knowing somehow that her life was at a changing point and that the images, laughable though they were at present, would one day be inexpressibly dear to her.

The second part of the cure, for all categories, was again supposed to be carried out in utmost privacy, upstairs for preference and not too close to the windows either; but after the humiliation of the scarves and segregation most of those afflicted rebelled, and to Carla's dismay – 'What *will* the Lessings think if they see?' – formed mutual de-egging groups in the garden, on the side where the acacias grew. '*Calma, amore mio,*' her husband Marco told her in mock reassurance. 'Nobody can see us, and if they do, they will merely think we have nits.' Which was of course exactly what Carla most feared.

Instead of a tragic summer, therefore, it was a mainly tetchy one, with points of comedy approaching authentic farce. What with the nursing of the measles victims and the campaign against the nits Irene had little time for grieving. Even the sight of Giuliano's bedroom window, tightly shuttered, and the occasional sound of his brothers and sisters playing the gramophone, didn't really bother her as much as she thought it would: she scarcely ever looked in the direction of the Lessing villa anyway if she could help it, and fortunately Caruso did not seem to be a particular favourite.

By late summer, Tommaso's and her plans for departure were more or less complete. Aunt Frances, unasked, had been busy string-pulling and what she called in a rather sinister fashion 'wangling things' on their behalf, and it looked as if, either thanks to this or regardless of it, temporary residence in the United Kingdom was going to be granted them without much trouble. The laws on nationality had been altered recently, and although no promises were given, Irene was led to understand in her correspondence with the Home Office that once she was back in England and had relinquished her Italian passport there was a good chance she would get her British one back again. On which – Tommaso consenting – she could then put the children, as a step towards their future citizenship.

This news came as a relief, because the summer did indeed bring changes to the world scene, all of them negative. July saw the first sliding of the regime towards an overt anti-Semitism with the publication of the Manifesto della Razza. A few weeks later came a law forbidding the enrolment of Jewish children in state schools, followed after a month's interval by another, banning all Jews from holding public office. These measures, bad enough in themselves, were given an even more frightening connotation by Maurice, who in a late-night telephone call to the villa begged Irene to note, not the laws, but the spirit in which they had been introduced. Had she heard Mussolini's explanations in that regard? Cobbled, embarrassed, apologetic almost. It was clear he wasn't introducing them out of ideological conviction but out of a desire to ingratiate himself with his new lord and master: they were, so to speak, his wedding present to Hitler, his pledge of wifely submission. 'What can I give you, Adolf, to prove my love?' 'Ah, dear Benito, if you really love me, give me your Jews on a platter of silver.'

This happened on the 2nd of September. Ten days later the situation in Czechoslovakia, festering all summer, worsened dramatically. So dramatically in fact that it seemed to Tommaso and Irene that they had already left it too late and that their departure, from imminent, had suddenly become impossible. Their plans to travel to England in early October remained unchanged, but at the same time acquired a sort of halo of unreality: the tickets and other papers, which Irene had been in the habit of thumbing through each morning with obsessive care to make sure none had gone missing overnight, were shoved unconcernedly into a drawer; she no longer woke up to find her mind tabulated like a laundry list – things done, things to do, things to take, things to leave; and her suitcases and trunk, already partially packed, she slid into a corner and covered with a spare bedspread. Deep down inside her the worrying was probably still going on, doubled, even trebled, but the surface result was one of dreamy unconcernedness: I am still here, in the place I love, with the people I love, the sun is still shining and there are no warships in sight, let me make the best of it.

Silvia seemed to share her mood – not of optimism, for it was anything but, but of care shelved, care suspended. When, like a colony of startled rabbits heading for the warren, the family began to make moves for a rapid return to Florence on the grounds that the wireless reception was better there and they would not feel so cut off and out of touch, she sauntered into Irene's bedroom, still dressed defiantly in her beach gear, and suggested that the pair of them ignore the alarm and remain where they were for the time being. 'If these are to be our last days of peace, then they might as well *be* peace, don't you agree? Besides, I'm not at all convinced that Florence *is* safer than Forte: I think the children would be better off here. Whatever happens. We've got the mill and the dairy close by, we've got the figs and the tomatoes in the Fontana, we could even plant potatoes. Oh, let's stay, Irene, do let's, just for a bit longer at any rate. Until the weather breaks.'

Or until the world breaks. The moment she heard them, Silvia's words seemed to Irene to have the authority and rightness of those of an oracle: now that flight was no longer possible (and in a sense how glad she was that it was no longer possible), this was of course the place they should be. Hadn't she always thought this, from the outset, that she could bear anything here? Come through any trial unscathed? And hadn't this so far been the case? Let them stay on then and see if they couldn't weather whatever tempest was in store.

CHAPTER XX

It was only much later that Irene came to think of this period as the Munich Crisis, meaning by it what other people did. For her, like everyone else, it was a time of intense underlying fear, but the critical aspect, the dreadful sick-making pendulum swing between war and peace, catastrophe and safety, hardly affected her at all. As far as she was concerned war was already on and the flight to England was off; it was a question of how to survive and plan ahead for survival. In fact, had it not been for a parallel crisis in her own life – short, messy, regrettable but never regretted – she would probably have looked back on those last September days spent in the villa with Silvia, Assunta, Carmela and the children (the perfect group, as she had always maintained), as extraordinarily happy ones.

And even with both crises to account for, goodness they did have fun. Against the onset of a food shortage which none of them save Assunta yet took seriously, they picked and bottled the last of the tomatoes, strung out the September yield of figs in the sun to dry, went blackberry picking in the hills and came back stained and scratched and laden, to boil their booty into jam in great bubbling iron cauldrons set out in rows on the top of the stove. They even hired Achille and his *carrozza* for a day and went high up into the mountains to look for chestnuts. (To make marrons glacés, in Silvia and Irene's intentions, but here Assunta put her foot down; far too wasteful of sugar: to make ordinary old chestnut flour as a stand-by. It was the only disagreement they had, and it didn't last long because there weren't any chestnuts as it turned out, only empty husks. 'These peasants,' Assunta commented scornfully, as if their own purposes were quite other, 'they'll lay their hands on anything!' The villa, inside and out, smelt of fruit and sweetness and abundance brought properly under control. Nobody was bored, nobody quarrelled, not even the children: like their elders, they were too caught up in the light-hearted urgency of the work at hand.

'We ought to get the mattresses seen to while we still can get the wool,' Assunta announced one morning. 'That's what the Padrona would have done if she was still alive.' And, it being more of a decree than an announcement, their activities over the next week were duly complicated (but also calmed because he was a very soothing man) by the presence of Signor Campanaro, the mattrress-maker, who set up his portable *bottega* in the central space of the garden where the knitting-circle had used to form, using the chairs to prop his work on, and combed his way systematically and unhurriedly through the stuffing of every mattress and pillow in the house: opening up the ticking, taking out the wool, spreading it on a sheet, smoothing it into neat fat skeins, adding whatever was necesssary to make up for lost volume, and then packing it back into its freshly washed cover again. Fluff flew everywhere, even through the kitchen window and on to the surface of the setting jam, and the whole process seemed to Irene to create more trouble than it was worth, but Assunta soon put her right about this: the standing of a household, she said, meaning from the sound of it just as much the moral standing as the financial, was to be judged by the regularity with which this operation of bedding-renewal was carried out. By their tickings ye shall know them.

Irene, a little uncertain now of her position in the household (after all, the half-packed cases were still there, under the sheet, the passports and tickets were still in the drawer), left the organizational side of things to Silvia and Assunta, and accepted along with the children a lot of humble outdoor chores, like skinning tomatoes and making onion plaits and rinsing and drying jars in the Fontana.

A choice not without its consequences because it was while she was engaged on this last task, one early sundrenched afternoon towards the very end of the month, that her private crisis (or muddle, or misadventure: it was too undignified really to qualify as a crisis) was set in motion. Not by any real cause nor for any real reason, but by the persuasive force of what philosophers would call 'the argument from illusion'. By a trick, in short. Holding up one of the jars against the light to check for moisture (because Assunta had warned that even the smallest patch of damp was prejudicial to the bottling process and could result in food-poisoning and terrible bomb-like explosions of both jars and people), Irene saw, slightly deformed by the shape of the glass but none the less unmistakable, the figure of Giuliano, standing only a few yards away from her on the other side of the netting. The foliage of the creepers was already withering, so she saw him clearly, jar-base notwithstanding. And he saw her, and did his old, slightly Prussian trick of jerking up his head and starting to attention, causing her whole world to come to an abrupt standstill.

For a moment, before logic caught up with her, she felt nothing but happiness. Happiness so total that it must still have been readable on her face when she lowered the jar and found herself looking into the porcine, but very interested, very intent, eyes of Giuliano's cousin, the son of the Admiral's sister.

She looked back, trying to deal with her insides which felt like the wool of one of Signor Campanaro's mattresses: in need of drastic reordering. Of course it was the cousin, she told herself in a mixture of anger and contempt for both of them, who else could it have been? She ought to have known as much immediately. Admittedly she had fallen into the same trap before, but only when Giuliano had been alive and such a mistake was plausible. (And admittedly she had entertained a kind of ghost fantasy about Giuliano once *after* his death, over the business of the Caruso song, but that too had been plausible in a very extreme sort of way.) Almost as if to punish herself for her gullibility she did not look away but went on staring closely into the counterfeit face in front of her, listing in her mind the similarities to the original and the discrepancies: same hair, different hairline; same skin colour, different bone structure; same nose, slightly fleshier; much greasier skin; no likeness in the eyes at all, could have been (in fact she had already noted this and identified which) those of another species. Only improvement, the teeth, which were more even and the front incisor unblemished. The rest was just a cruel parody.

Thou shalt not stare, or not that long: although Irene's intent this time round was purely observational, the commandment evidently still held good. The cousin – what *was* his name? Monica had told her once. Something Germanic and faintly ridiculous, rhyming with dodo. Bodo, that was right, Bodo – Bodo was staring back with an unmistakably receptive expression on his face. An intrigued, flattered, and what he perhaps intended to be flattering expression but was far too forthright to be so. He was giving her what Aunt Frances called the 'come hither look'. He had thought (understandably when you knew how hard-pushed young Italian males were to find casual partners for this sort of game) that with her stare she had sent out a first tentative signal of availability, and he was signalling back that he was ready to avail himself of whatever she had to offer.

Irritation, embarrassment, plus a sense of irony so stinging that it made her eyes water as if she'd been handling onions again, swept through Irene in quick succession. She knew perfectly well that if she wished to clear up the misunderstanding (and she must clear up the misunderstanding) the moves on her part were two: she could either go right up close to the wire-netting on the instant and begin speaking to this Bodo creature in a spirit of open friendliness, 'How nice to meet you at last. How is your aunt? Please give her my regards when you see her,' that sort of thing; or else she could turn her back on him curtly without a word and avoid crossing eyes with him for the next couple or so times they met.

She knew, but for some reason she was at a loss to understand she did neither of these things. Instead, as if she had become a glove puppet, she thought afterwards, and some other creature was inside her controlling her movements, she smiled: a slow, dulcet smile, almost a simper. *You* come hither. Then, her eyes still holding Bodo's which were becoming very bright and twinkly now, she placed her clean jars upside down in the crate she used for carrying and backed slowly away from the netting, not turning away nor cancelling her smile until she was a good ten metres distant and her expression (now changed to one of puzzled distaste) could no longer be seen.

Things moved very quickly from here. Quickly and inexorably and extremely quietly. No so much, Irene sometimes thought, out of a need to conceal her movements from the others (which she wasn't entirely successful at anyway), as from a need to conceal them from herself. She didn't seem to want her mind to catch up with her, to discover what her body was doing. Because the simile of the glove puppet was consoling but misleading: rather than an alien force taking charge of her body it would have been more honest to say that her body routed all other forces and took charge of itself.

That evening saw her taking up her old place at Silvia's window and engaging in the ritual game of darts with her new partner: catching, throwing, aiming, returning, scoring up the hits. As over the business of the smile, her purposes were hidden from her, and although a small voice inside her condemned what she was doing as sad and pointless and even rather sordid, the rest of her took no notice and went wilfully ahead with the game. With such covert participation, too, that to her surprise she found her clothes drenched with sweat when she went to bed and her heart hammering so hard that she was unable to sleep for hours.

The darts found their target and did their work, and next morning, transfixed by their invisible barbs like a profane and unedifying Saint Sebastian, Bodo was there on the seabound path that led through the pine wood, waiting for her: as obedient to her summons, if not more so, than Giuliano himself had been. Italian men tended, nearly all of them, in Irene's experience, to have a high regard for their own desirability, particularly where foreign women were concerned, but even so she was amazed by the matter of factness with which this very ordinary-looking young man seemed to accept her (surely a little untypical) enthusiasm for his person. Did he really think a leer through a fence was sufficient to conquer her? Someone of her calibre? And a leer, what was more, coming from someone like him? Apparently he did. And apparently, in her case at least, he was one hundred per cent right.

She never cared to recall what they said to one another by way of preamble; presumably, their backgrounds being what they were, they must have made some formal attempt at small talk, but if so it must have been very small indeed in all senses, seeing that by the time they had completed the short walk to the beach they had dispensed with formality entirely and made what amounted to a definite assignment.

Like Giuliano (and yet so horribly unlike that the comparison did not bear drawing), once the meeting had been agreed on Bodo was impatient. 'Tonight? Can you come tonight? I will wait for you by the gate; my uncle locks it at night but I will open it for you. What time will you come? Come early, please – as soon as it is safe.' He went on in this vein, speaking of lights and signals and counter-signals, until Irene, with a curtness she felt he must have noticed but did not appear to resent, cut him short. The breakdown in communications between her mind and body, which had started with the episode of the smile in the Fontana and worsened ever since, seemed to be more or less complete now, and the only feeling she was able consciously to register was one of equal, perhaps even greater impatience: whatever her business was with this accommodating young man, it evidently had to brought quickly to its conclusion.

In contrast to their opening exchange, the closing one stuck in her memory clearly ever afterwards. To shame her, yes, undoubtedly, but also to bewilder and intrigue and indeed at times fascinate her. With a gesture she had never seen used before and yet had no trouble recognizing, Bodo lifted his fist to chest-level, wrist turned outwards, towards her, flexed it and made a rapid piston movement: backwards, forwards, backwards, forwards. Then he said distinctly, his face wreathed in a delighted smile, 'Tonight then, *a stasera*. Chucky, chucky, chucky!' And she, slowly and inexpertly – it was one of the things that most amused Tommaso, her inability to gesticulate like a proper Italian – raised her own arm and made exactly the same movement back at him; not only undisturbed by the vulgarity of the transaction but appeased by it, as if it was exactly this she had been seeking.

So much for the glove-puppet theory. She knew perfectly well, then, what she was about to do? Well, by the time midnight had come and the lights in both villas were off, and she had taken note of this with secretarial precision and begun creeping down the stairs with her shoes in her hand, she knew more or less what the visit would result in, at least on the physical plane: as she had once said to Giuliano in complete truthfulness, she was not one to go back on her word. And that went for gestures as well. But not really until she was outside in the garden, already walking towards the gate, did the knowledge become explicit, propositional, something she could formulate in words; and by that time her body had outrun her, was already sweating again and trembling and hastening towards the tryst.

Strangely (Maurice would doubtless have said not so strangely, but then she never told Maurice, never really felt she needed to), the only guilt Irene ever felt afterwards was guilt towards – of all people – Bodo. She went through with things and slept with him, she spoke civilly, almost amicably, to him in the aftermath of sex, she spoke just as civilly to him next day on the beach, albeit to re-decline a second appointment; in the reigning system of values she had not only done him no offence but emerged from their commerce as debtor. And yet whenever she thought of him in years to come (which thankfully was less and less often), his image in her mind would invariably be accompanied by a kind of scroll or caption over its head bearing the Kantian maxim: Never treat a fellow human being as a means, but always as an end. Bodo may have ended up with a very different impression (and if he did, so much the better), but the fact remained that in the light of her own conscience she had made use of him, practically, briefly, like a paper napkin, and then cast him aside. And this was wrong, no matter how many rights results from it.

Her wrongs towards Tommaso and Giuliano, on the other

hand, she always considered as fully atoned for by the very action through which she committed them. The moment the waiting figure of Bodo reached out to touch her (only to take her hand at this stage: he too had a few ignition problems to begin with, probably linked to sheer inablility to believe his luck), her body, which had thus far behaved as if seeped from head to foot in Spanish fly or some other potent aphrodisiac, went dead on her and remained dead in all the key places throughout.

He led her into the covered space under the terrace where the ping-pong table stood. It was, she realized, the first time she had ever set foot in Giuliano's territory. (Was this, then, the reason she had come? To be near Guiliano? If so, it struck her that she could hardly have chosen a more perverse and destructive way.) She would have liked to linger there a little and see in the moonlight what their own garden looked like from this side, and make sure she had remembered to shut the dog in when she closed the front door, but Bodo seemed anxious for them to enter the house.

'My uncle walks about a lot at night,' he explained. 'Doesn't sleep very well, you know, since the *disgrazia*.'

Irene concentrated on the first part of this sentence to avoid thinking about the second. Barring the removal of her shoes on the staircase, which she had carried out more from a sense of courtesy to the other sleepers than anything else, the possibility of discovery by a third party had not really occurred to her: she had been too busy foiling self-discovery to bother about the other kind. The mention of the Admiral, however, made it suddenly real to her. She was struck by the enormity and at the same time utter futility of the risk she was taking, and her trembling increased so violently that her teeth began to chatter. But still she had no thought other than to go ahead.

Holding her fast by the hand, Bodo led her round to the back of the villa where there was another outside ramp of stairs leading straight to the second storey. So they were not to enter the part of the villa inhabited by the Lessing family at all. Irene registered this fact with relief as far as the noctambulant figure of the Admiral was concerned, but also with a certain disappointment, similar to that she had felt on the day of the missed visit of condolence: closer than this to Giuliano's home environment, it seemed she would never come.

It was her last thought related to Giuliano for some time, indeed it was almost her last thought related to anyone or anything. From that moment on she donned what was in effect a pair of mental blinkers, shutting out from her mind everything but the present, and a narrow segment of it at that. She followed Bodo up the stairs, through the door, through a passage, and into a very small, bleak bedroom with an unmade-up bed in it. (Lumpy mattress, very inferior ticking: her eye had become quite expert by now. What a shame she could say nothing of her discovery to Assunta.)

'The maid's room,' he said apologetically. 'Or where the maid sleeps when she's here. She's in Florence at the moment with my mother. I share with my brother, you see, and – '

'Quite,' Irene said, in a voice devoid of any expression, unbacked by any feelings whatsoever, except possibly a mild return of her earlier impatience.

Bodo looked at her worriedly, taking her briefness for a sign of her having taken offence, and then looked round the room again. 'I suppose we could use my mother's room if you prefer.'

'Good lord, no,' Irene said, involuntarily loudly, and then checked herself. 'No, I mean no, this is fine. Absolutely fine. *Va benissimo.*'

She said it truthfully, quite without irony. As over the business of the 'chucky, chucky', the squalor of their surroundings for some reason suited her purposes very well. It was Bodo now who seemed to think that the scene was in need of some kind of ennoblement, some touch of grace. He opened a cupboard and began rummaging around inside it on his knees. In search, Irene imagined, of a sheet or counterpane.

To speed up matters she knelt beside him, and her proximity evidently gave him back his courage. An incalculable amount of time later – it might have been anything from ten to forty minutes – they were lying side by side on the bed, still minus a counterpane, having accomplished their coincidental but very divergent business together. They had not spoken at all, save for an enquiry towards the end from Irene about what contraceptive method he intended to employ, and a slightly plaintive, 'Withdrawal – if I have to,' from Bodo; who had thus aroused the first stirring of guilt in Irene on his behalf, and had in fact ended up discharging himself, after a blotched attempt to part her sphincter, in her mouth.

'I really would have preferred to stay just where I was,' he admitted, unappreciatively to Irene's way of thinking, as she got up to put her clothes on. 'Italian girls will sometimes let you use their mouths or their back passages if they like you enough, but it's very rare to be allowed to use the proper place.' (Something in her behaviour must still have been perplexing him, she decided, because after a few clumsy attempts at the salacious and the tender, he was now speaking to her neutrally, more like he would to another man.) 'The trouble is, though, even if you're married you can do that only certain times of the month. Perhaps' – his voice from neutral became a trifle wistful – 'a little later on . . . mmn? How long are you staying?'

Irene stiffened slightly and wiped her mouth on the hem of her skirt as she drew it over her head. With the replacement of her clothes her body seemed to be coming back to her, returning under her control. She could see now what it had been up to in her absence, feel it too, and all she wanted now was to get away from the scene of aberration as quickly and permanently as possible. 'I don't know,' she replied. 'Not very long, I shouldn't think, perhaps a few more days.' Then, remembering Silvia's convenient formula, and the fact that rain was shortly forecast, 'We'll stay until the weather breaks, most likely. Then we'll be off, back to Florence.'

Bodo gave her another puzzled look: conquered women were notoriously clinging, and yet here was one of them, not only not clinging but actually straining to get away. 'I should think your husband keeps a close hold over you in Florence, doesn't he?' he asked, not in the nicest of voices.

'Yes,' said Irene tersely. She did not like to hear him mention Tommaso, not even in an indirect way.

'I thought as much. Pity. Pity we can't meet up there, I mean. Or can we?'

Irene shook her head, and he nodded in response, accepting her veto immediately although it evidently went against his wishes. He is not a bad creature, she thought. It is I who have forced him to behave badly, or what he thinks is badly, but he is not really a bad creature in himself at all.

As soon as she had finished dressing she headed for the door with what she hoped was not too great a show of speed. One thing remained still undone, but she didn't know this, or know what it was, until she found herself hesitating on the threshold, searching her mind for the reason for her sudden reluctance to leave the room. It was a link, that was it, some link between this and the earlier situation had to be forged. Otherwise, on purely superstitious grounds but real ones none the less, it would all have been in vain. 'By the way,' she said lightly, 'you look rather like your cousin, did anyone ever tell you?'

'Like which cousin?'

Of course, she was forgetting, he had so many. 'Like the one that was drowned.'

His face lit up with pleasure. 'Like Giuliano? Really? I'm glad you say that, I wish I did.'

'Well, you do.' And before other thoughts came to him Irene shut the door behind her and slipped out quietly into the night. Really quiet, inside and out, for the first time in – how long was it since she caught her first glimpse of Giuliano? – in nearly six and a half years.

An American friend of Irene's, to whom she told the story many years later, called it very aptly 'laying the ghost'. Irene herself, however, preferred never to rationalize, not even to this superficial extent. She just put the whole thing behind her and went ahead with her life, happily, peacefully (war notwithstanding) from that moment on.

In mid-October, she, Tommaso and the children transferred themselves, as planned, to England. The parting from the family was heartrending: there had been much speculation about German weaponry during the weeks of the Munich crisis and nobody seemed very sure any more that England was a safe place to be. 'Go further now that you are going,'

Maurice urged Irene when he came to say goodbye. 'That channel of yours is just a puddle.' 'Go to America – Canada – Australia,' Aunt Tita seconded dashingly, earning herself a lot of black looks.

One thing, however, happened to alleviate the sadness from Irene's point of view. A gift, or restitution of a gift, all the more precious for being entirely unlooked for and undeserved. The night before they left Silvia came into her bedroom while she was finishing her packing and sat down on the bed, the old conspiratorial look of the heyday of their friendship back on her face. 'There was one thing I wanted to ask you,' she said, lighting a cigarette and following the smoke with her eyes. 'That night at Forte when you came in so late – I was awake, you know. The dog woke me, he was barking, I had to get up and let him in. Where were you? What had you been up to?'

Automatically Irene began to offer some bland excuse about insomnia, but then something in Silvia's expression – a shuttering of her face in disappointment or resignation – made her change her mind and tell the truth instead. Whole, exact, and unmitigated by explanations because it was part of the essence of the story that she had none to put forward.

She was never really sure how much or how deeply Silvia understood. Her reaction could have been determined by one of several things: tact, kindness, admiration for Irene's bravado, relief at her moral downfall, or just what it seemed: merriment pure and simple. Anyway, that kind of understanding didn't matter. All that mattered was that the other kind of understanding was re-established between them as if by magic, and from that moment onward the crack in their friendship mended, vanished, simply ceased to exist. When Irene had finished speaking Silvia was silent for a second or two, then she rocked slowly on to her back, holding her knees to her chest, and began to laugh until the bed shook. 'I don't believe it!' she kept murmuring between spasms, smoke and ash flying everywhere. 'What a dotty, crazy thing to do, Irene! After all these years of sacrifice at the altar of marital fidelity, to go and leap into bed with Bodo at a moment's notice – with *Bodo*, if you please! – I just don't believe it!'

Irene was always a little uneasy with this comic finale to her drama. She had imposed it herself, but only in the flesh, never in the heart. Even when she came to realize that Maurice had spoken truly, and that love was an achievement, not a datum, and that in this sense it was indeed Tommaso she had loved all along and always would, she continued to keep a small space in her heart for the other taste of love, the other experience – like a romantically inclined market gardener who keeps a tiny flower patch in his huge and flourishing vegetable garden. Nevertheless, in future years, whenever she found herself missing Silvia, which despite many visits on both sides was often, it was in the pose of that night that she liked to remember her: curled up on the bed with her feet in the air, laughing her head off over what until that moment had been, and had looked like remaining, an incurably sad affair.